AUTOGRAPH PAGE

Join my blog and order an autographed copy of **Flicted** at *AJKush.com*. You can also order the Kindle, NOOK, or paperback version from Amazon.com, BarnesAndNoble.com, or anywhere books are sold.

This is a work of fiction. Any references or similarities to actual events, locales, real people, living or dead are intended to give the novel a sense of reality. Any similarity in other names, characters, places and incidents is entirely coincidental.

New Paradigm Education Solutions
P.O. Box 831918
Stone Mountain, GA 30083

FLICTED copyright © 2017 *AJ Kush*

ISBN: 978-0-692985045

First Printing: December 2017
Printed in the United States of America

10 9 8 7 6 5 4 3 2 1

Wholesale Order contact: New Paradigm Education Solutions at AJKush@gmail.com

is dedicated to my daughters Omega and Zipporah. *I wanted to show you that you can do anything you put your mind to. This book is a testament to that truth. I love you eternally.*

I would also like to dedicate this work to the loving memory of my father, H.C. Jones; Kenyatta Washington; April Jenkins; and Darryl Simmons. May all of you Rest In Power.

APPRECIATION PAGE

First, I would like to thank my mom for having the hope and belief that I would be great. I may not have always listened at the time but you planted good seeds that eventually grew. I love you for that and for instilling a strong work ethic in me.

Thanks to my beautiful Wife for listening to me talk about this novel and every step of the process a thousand times without complaining. I appreciate you and all that you do.

Special shout out to my homeboy Jarrelle Evans. He believed in the vision from the beginning and fought to help me make this a reality. Even when I had doubts, he believed.

Thanks to Jermaine Simmons, Veronica Jones, Darius Harris, Patricia Grant, Mark Johnson, Marquis Jones, Khary Amerson, Rashad Taylor, Dwhontany Wilder, Keir Chapple, Jessica Bassey, Charles Singleton, Kameelah

4

FLICTED

Martin, LaDamon Douglas, Street Smart Youth Project
(Monique & Tomica), Lashawna Rivers, Jason Louder,
Brian Price, Stephanie Fort, Chalea Jenkins-Ayers, Derrick
Figures, Rasheem Nurse, Quamilius Scott, Ahmad Taylor,
Tara Schuster, Antione Youmans, Barry Sears, Timothia
Johnson, Dee Whitfield, Shalita Douglass, Robert Scott,
Keith Fripp, Roderick Williams, Musa Mateen, Zakiyya
Broadie, Craig Gordan, Mike Meyers, Eric Hammond,
DeKeisha Bridgeforth, Patry Morris, Greg Haywood,
Brian Roberson, Earl Redman, Shayla Grant, Courtney
Shakesphere, ViaKristi Varnell, Andre Mountain, Marcian
Knowles, Derrin Moore, and all the other countless friends
and family who took time to read earlier versions, listen to
my ideas, and give your opinion about everything related
to this project. This work is a reflection of you and your
honest feedback. Your encouragement propelled me
towards success.

To all the professionals who assisted in editing and
mentorship. Jihad Uhuru (bruh, I don't believe in
coincidences; we linked at the perfect time. Many thanks
for your expert advice and ultrabionic writing skills),
Victoria Christopher Murry (thanks for challenging me
and my writing to be great), Nicole Twum-Baah, and Dara
Mathis. This work could not have come to fruition without
your service.

Lastly, I want to think every rapper I acknowledged in
this work for their creativity and inspiration. Big Daddy
Kane, KRS-One, Heavy D, EST of Three Times Dope,
Wise Intelligent, Steady B, LL Cool J, Public Enemy,
Monie Love, Salt-N-Pepa, Young & Restless, Jungle
Brothers, MC Lyte, Queen Latifah, Young MC, 2 Live

Crew, Biz Markie, Slick Rick, New Edition, Digital Underground, N.W.A., A Tribe Called Quest, De La Soul, YZ, 3rd Bass, Rob Base, D.O.C., Geto Boys, The Fresh Prince, and Poison Clan. To whom much is given, much is required. I could never fully repay what Hip hop did for me; however, this is my humble offering of thanks.

We are afflicted in every way,
but not crushed; perplexed, but not
driven to despair…

-2 Corinthians 4:8

April 1990

Walking through her hotel room felt unbelievable. Every step I took, I shook with heart-pounding tremors. I knew her intentions by the way she raised her eyebrows. Then she wrapped her arms around me and pulled me closer. As she began to slowly place her lips on mine, all I could manage was to drool. I had no idea how to kiss the way she did. Still, her eyes summoned me closer. What should I do? Was it real? Was she playing with my head? What about the note?

Hold up, I'm going much too fast. For you to understand just how flicted this was, I need to start from the beginning.

CHAPTER 1

GET IT GIRL

"I been looking at you for
a while, with your big brown
eyes and your pretty smile.
Every guy calls you sexy, but
your man is weak.
He can't satisfy you, baby;
I'm your freak."

-2 Live Crew

August 1989

It was an electric afternoon in August filled with blue skies and I was still on summer vacation. Everyone was outside. It was so hot, it seemed like it rained gasoline and now the sun was setting us on fire. You could literally see the heat radiating off the ground.

Around the corner not too far from my cousin's house, some dudes were sitting on top of cars sipping beers, little kids were playing tag, and the sounds of laughter filled the block of this small Alabama town called Andalusia.

My cousin, Stick, and I were shooting ball in the streets. It was one of those days when we owned the streets since not too many cars were coming through.

I passed the ball to Stick and he passed it back to me. I dribbled it back and forth with both hands, the ball bouncing between my legs, my thoughts far away from the game we were playing. Now that we were both headed to the eighth grade, we talked about more than just playing ball.

"You gon' shoot or hold the ball 'til the streetlights come on?" Stick asked, his hands ready to play defense.

Everybody thought Stick was older than me, probably because of the peach fuzz growing on his upper lip, but we were the same age.

"Man, cuz, I keep thinking about this girl I saw," I dribbled the ball.

"Dez, there is always a girl you saw," he teased.

"Nah, but this is different." I shook my head. "I saw her at that church revival they made me go to last week."

"What's her name?"

"I wish I knew. She's so right, though. She's dark brown, slim, and she got a nice little boonkie on her."

"Boonkie…?"

"Oh, I forgot y'all say booty out here."

"And you got the nerve to call us country," Stick smirked.

"Bama is country, you know everybody here still wear Jheri curls."

"Whatever, I still don't know the girl you talking 'bout. Why don't you just ask Ree-ree who she is? That girl know everybody."

I looked at Stick like he bumped his head on the goal post.

"Maybe I don't want our big-mouth cousin to know who I like."

"You not scared, are you?" he asked.

"Nah." I stopped dribbling for a sec. "Are you?"

Stick flexed his bicep. "A lot of times, I don't have to say nothing. Girls see these muscles and come to me."

For me, this was not the case. I was nervous and a bit nerdy around girls. One side of me wanted to tell the whole world how I felt, but the other part of me couldn't open my mouth for shit.

I dribbled the ball and took another shot. "Stick, that's my third shot in a row. Buckets."

"Step back some, you see that line right there?" He pointed to a mark behind the three-point line. "That's where Robert Horry used to hit from."

"Robert who?"

"Horry. He was one of the best 'round here, he plays for Bama now."

"Right here?" I looked at him like he must be exaggerating.

"Yep. Shoot."

"Alright check it, it's five seconds left – Dez Allen with the ball, ladies and gentlemen. Three...two...one..." I heaved up a long shot.

"Briiiick, and you lose again." Stick laughed. "It's getting dark. Let's go get ready."

I wiped away the sweat dripping from my forehead, before asking, "Get ready for what?"

"You forget already? It's skate night, which means plenty of girls and I mean plenty."

"Dag, that's right. Let's go."

We damn near broke our ankles running up the lane to his house, as fast as we could.

****

Friday night in Andalusia meant skate night at the local rink. Dazzling lights, loud bass music, and tender ronis everywhere. We put on our outfits in record time, then waited for his mom to drop us off.

"Let's see what's on the tube, my mom isn't ready yet," Stick said, feeling in the cracks of the chair for the remote. Flipping through channels, he stopped on BET. "You seen *Do the Right Thing* yet?"

"Nah, but this "Fight the Power" video is hard as hell.

"*'Cause I'm black and I'm proud and I'm amped – most of my heroes don't appear on no stamps.*"

I rapped along with the music.

"Dez, you still be trying to rap? You the only person I know with every rap known to man memorized."

My face looked like a rag being wrung out. "Trying to rap?" Slightly offended, I cleared my throat to spit.

"*It's the D to the E-Z. I invent style. Look cousin, I get the numbers to dial. So smile, sit back and lighten up, your bald-headed girlfriend got no buuutt...*"

He sucked his teeth so hard he almost cracked a couple. "Man, you didn't write that."

"I know, I just made it up." I pointed to my head and wiggled my neck.

Stick smirked, "I guess you can rap then… a lil' bit."

FLICTED

When his mom dropped us at the rink, the line was wrapped 'round the building with tons of people waiting to get in. People bumped and shoved until security threatened to close the doors for good if we didn't calm down. The latest jams from Miami, along with "Push It" and "Supersonic," blared through the speakers making some people dance in line.

Everything was perfect when we entered the rink known as THE PALACE, and for three hours the outside world ceased to exist.

"It's about to get crazaaay in here," Stick shouted.

"Oh my god, bruh, I'm in heaven. That's her, that's her...that's the girl from church," I said, yanking on his arm.

She had on a stylish, turquoise halter top with biking shorts under a pair of cut up jeans. She glided around the rink like a natural. Her long ponytail gave her an innocent allure though her mannerisms were all woman.

"Wow, that's who you talking about? That's Jade, man," Stick said, obviously impressed with my taste. "You would pick one of the finest girls in Andalusia. She's pretty, you sure you got that game for her?"

"Watch this." I took off skating.

"Watch what?" he said in disbelief. "I thought you could barely skate, you better slow your ass down."

Despite my lack of skating experience, I wanted to do something to catch her attention. In my mind, I saw myself skating backwards next to her with my arms crossed, but instead, I whizzed past her, out of control and into the hardest wall ever. I straight up busted my ass. Unfortunately for me, Jade saw that. She glanced over as I attempted to get up, but slipped and fell again. I wasn't

13

sure if she recognized me from church, so I laid face down 'til Stick came over.

"What were you thinking?" he said, putting both hands on his head. "You look flicted as hell."

That word. Flicted. It was a word we used over in Savannah, Georgia, when I was growing up. To me, it meant that something was weird or funny looking. I wasn't sure if it was a Southern thing, or something all black people used at the time, but the way we used it in regular conversation was crazy to me. It came from the word afflicted, which meant an illness or deep emotional pain. I wondered how a word could be that funny and yet so serious.

"Dag, cuz, I don't even know." I wanted to fade into the ground.

"You coulda' just walked up to her and talked, why a stunt?"

"It wasn't a stunt, I just wanted her to look my way...before I said something."

"Okay, I need you to play this off and walk away nice and easy." He laughed. "Let's go back to the dance floor, maybe I can introduce you to her later."

For the next few hours, I played video games and choked down popcorn. I stayed way out of sight until the main mix of the night started.

"Are y'all party people ready?" the DJ howled. "If you can't dance, go home right now. This is for the girls with moves; that want you to know... it's alright to..."

Get, Get, Get, Get it Girl
Get, Get, Get, Get it Girl

When those claps hit and the bass dropped, every girl in The Palace rushed to the dance floor. I knew the words backwards and forwards to 2 Live Crew's anthem; it was my jam. As puberty coursed through my body, I had to see how Jade danced. I pushed through the crowd, peeked over a few shoulders, and there she was.

She bent over, dropped down, and spread her feathers for the crowd to gaze. She was mesmerizing. I waited 'til the DJ played the next song, then I walked up to introduce myself.

"Hey Jade, we got off to a bad start...well, actually I got off to a–"

"Hold up, aren't you in the sixth grade? Why don't you call me when you grow a bit," she joked while pretending to fall. "Oh yeah, that big orange thing on your skate is called a brake, use it."

Sixth grade? I'm in the eighth. I thought to myself, but I was speechless. There was nothing quite like making a fool of yourself.

Stick, overhearing the whole thing, walked up from behind. "Don't sweat it, cuz, it's too many girls to be upset over one. Plus, I heard her breath be staaank."

I knew he made that up to make me feel better, but rejection sucked. I was a young boy still wet behind the ears and skate night as well as my chance at love was officially over.

The next morning after choking down breakfast, we sat at the table and talked about what had happened at the rink. "I can't stop thinking about last night," I said. "I feel so damn lame..."

I was looking up at the ceiling so Stick tapped me on the head to bring me back to reality. "You should feel lame. It seemed like you were in love; you had that look in your eyes. 'Oooh Jade...'" He caressed my hand.

"Naaah, not that easy, you tryin' to be funny, but what if I was...?"

His eyes shot open. "Was what, in love?"

I nodded.

"Then, I'd probably laugh and watch your heart get broken again," Stick pointed out.

"So, if a guy really *lov-* I mean, like a girl, you think he's soft?"

"I don't know, but I ain't falling in love with nobody anytime soon. Let's go hoop. Maybe now you can keep up since Ms. Thang dissed you." With that he popped me on the head and I chased him all the way to the court.

My dad was supposed to pick me up around noon, so I had about three hours left. I figured I'd take my mind off everything that happened at the rink and just play ball. When my dad arrived in his trusty red Oldsmobile, we were dirt tired. After he talked with Stick's mom, we put my luggage in the car and drove to his house in Enterprise.

Since the age of six, I had spent every summer vacation with my dad in Alabama. Each summer, he would pick me up from my home in Savannah, Georgia, where I stayed with my mother and stepfather, and we would drive the many hours to Alabama. While in Alabama, either he or my stepmother would take me to Andalusia to visit with family, which was why I had been staying with Stick for the last two weeks.

"What have you all been up to?" my dad asked me on our way home.

Pulling myself from a daydream about the rink, I gulped down some soda and started, "Uhh, we played basketball, video games, and stayed up late...the usual stuff. Oh, and...we went to the skating rink last night," I said while writing the word sucker on the window with my finger. "Hey Pop, I need some new sneakers."

"Is that the first thing you're gonna ask me? No, how are you doing? How's life? None of that?"

I grinned. "Well, you know, that's what I meant to say."

"Yeah, right. Y'all went to church a lot?" he asked.

"Yep, the first week they had revival every night I was there. That was a lot of church." I wiped my forehead like I was tired.

"So, you didn't like it?"

"Well, it's not like I had a choice whether to go or not. I guess it was okay."

Halfway into our hour-long ride, I flipped through radio stations until *Parents Just Don't Understand* came on.

I peeped at him to see if he was catching the lyrics.

"So, this is the kind of bullshit you like, huh?" He looked at me like I stole something. "You know if you keep listening to that bullshit, you're going to talk like that."

"You think so?"

"I know so," he said adjusting his rear view mirror.

"I know you really like Hip hop," I teased. "You just don't want to admit it."

"Boy, I listen to real music like Earth, Wind, and Fire and Teddy Pendergrass."

"I like some of that stuff, too, Pop, but you gotta stay hip. You can't be in 1989 talking about The Temptations like they're brand new."

"Yeah, yeah, I hear you," he said, just to brush me off.

After the drive from Andalusia to Enterprise, on a long empty country road, we finally pulled up to Dad's house. I could smell the chicken on the grill as soon as we got out of the car. I followed the smell to the backyard where I found my stepmom, Lydia, by the pool. She was sitting in her favorite lawn chair, one hand loosely holding a Benson & Hedges cigarette, the other holding a Bartles & Jaymes wine cooler.

Lydia reminded me of Willona from *Good Times*. She was always in an upbeat mood and she gave it to you straight.

"Hey, Lydia," I said, excited to be back.

She took a quick puff of her cigarette. "Hey, I heard you and Stick had a lot of fun. When I talked to Stick's mom, all she did was talk about y'all and that basketball."

"Yeah, I had a good time. We stayed up late almost every night." I flung my hand to push away the smoke. "What you been up to?"

"I hadn't been doing much, just trying to deal with all this heat. Ree-ree and her brother are here, they're inside changing to get in the pool.

"Ok, let me put my things up." When I came back out Ree-ree kept smiling at me. I knew she had something to say about the skating rink fiasco.

"Hey Dez, so you like that girl, Jade, at our church, huh?" she cornered me at the deep in the pool.

"Dag, Stick definitely wasn't supposed to tell you, mouth almighty."

"I don't have a big mouth." She cleared her throat. "I just like to know what's going on, lil' sixth grader."

18

"I knew that was coming. You still on the itty bitty titty committee though?" I rubbed my chest.

"That's not funny."

"Uuuh, yes, it is."

"Ooo, okay, look who finally got black now," she said while examining my arm.

"You trying to be funny about my tan – wait while I laugh."

"Look lil' Al B. Sure, everybody knows you needed some sun, don't act. I can get with you all day if you wanna talk junk." Her neck rolled in record speed.

After splashing water back and forth, we were gagging on chlorine and broke out laughing.

"You had enough of messing with me about my future wife?"

"For now," she said climbing out of the pool. "Seriously though, I don't think you're her type. She's kind of tall."

I shrugged my shoulders. "What's that got to do with it?"

"Well, some people look good together. You can't be a runt going with somebody twice your size."

"I ain't no damn runt."

"I know, I'm just sayin'."

I didn't take too kindly to light-skin or short jokes, but my cousin and I went back and forth all the time, so I really wasn't studdin' her.

"Do you even know how to talk to girls?" She looked at me suspiciously.

"Of course."

"Well don't be a jackass like most of these boys; they don't know what to say." Then, she began mimicking people. *"Hey fine looking, I like your booty. Or girl... let me get them digits with your fine ass.'* I get so tired of that junk. Remember to be yourself, cuz, and try to be sweet."

"Sweet…girls really like that romance type stuff?" I asked without a clue.

"Duh…yeah…take it from me, cuz, I know."

****

That night after the barbecue, I laid down on my bed and thought about what she said. I wanted to be "the man" when it came to girls, but I knew I had a lot to learn. Why was I so awkward? It wasn't like I was ugly. Maybe I needed some kind of love manual on what to say.

To take my mind off Jade, I thumbed through my old *Word Up!* magazine and there it was. Right next to the EPMD interview, there was a black heart with my name inside. It read, Dez -n- K with a big question mark. *Where in the heck did this come from? Was it one of my crazy friends back in Savannah playing a joke?*

Everybody had borrowed this magazine from me so it was hard to be sure. But maybe it was Kalia, the girl I had a crush on for the entire seventh grade. The same girl I told myself I wanted to marry and have fifty 'leven kids with although she was waaay out of my league.

I remembered the day she came up behind me, rubbed my shoulder and asked if she could see it. That was the first and only time she had spoken to me that entire year. If it was her, and I damn sure wanted it to be, my life was about to change.

CHAPTER 2

AIN'T NO HALF STEPPIN'

"Brain cells are lit. Ideas start
to hit. Next the formation of words
that fit. At the table I sit. Making it
legit. And when the pen hits the
paper, ahh shit."

-Big Daddy Kane

August 1989

The next morning, I woke up with my head plastered against the box fan in my room. Last night, I turned the fan on high and buried myself in a pile of blankets. Someone must have come in during the night and cut it off. Now, I felt dry and ashy like I had been abandoned in a desert. However, this was the day I was to return home.

Instead of my dad driving me back to Savannah like usual, my mom arrived with a male friend of hers whom I hadn't seen since I was about eight. This linky joker was my mother's suitor before she married my stepdad. So why-the-hell-was-he-here? Were my mom and stepdad having problems?

My mom came in loud as usual. "*Chile*, let me tell you," she started talking to my dad.

"What's going on, Betty?"

"I'm good except for the dumb folks at my job." They hugged each other. "They're trying to make me lose it. Every day I go to work it's something." She plopped down on the nearest sofa.

Yep, each story came complete with impersonations and sound effects to make sure you were listening. This was who she was and once she had you trapped in her stories, she would talk your head off. After an hour of doing just that, my dad's head was on the floor spinning.

Finally she looked at her watch. "Well, Derrick, you ready to go?"

"Yeah, I'ma miss ol' Bama, though," I said, patting my dad on the back. "Seriously, I appreciate everything. I had a great summer with you and Lydia."

"We enjoyed you too, son." He put his hand on my head.

"Make sure you get all them tapes," Lydia said.

My dad agreed. "Betty, that boy carry 'round music like he's a store."

"Huh, tell me about it." My mom looked at all the tapes I had bought over the summer and pretended to faint.

I grinned, then waved goodbye. At first, the trip back didn't seem so bad. I ran my mouth about the summer and my mom was glad to hear that I had a good time.

"You said you were in Anda who?" her friend asked.

"An-da-lu-sia," I said, pronouncing every syllable.

"Sounds like you had a good time. I used to love going to visit my folks in the country when I was your age. Say, Derrick, are you still smart?"

Nah, bruh, I'm dumb, I thought, looking up at the ceiling.

"I remember your mother telling me how you always make the honor roll. Keep it up, maybe you can get into Princeton or Harvard."

"Harvard, yeah...okay, just like you did," I mumbled.

For a while, no one had anything to say, so I let myself drift off to thoughts of Jade and that moment at the skating rink. What was I afraid of? Even when she joked that I was in the 6th grade, I should have shot back with something. Now, my only hope for love was a dumb ass note in my magazine.

After we stopped for a restroom break, I remembered the mix tape in my pocket. "Mama, can you pop this in?"

She rolled her eyes like a slot machine. "Jesus, not all that rappity rap." She knew her break from my music was over. EPMD, Ice-T, and Stetsasonic had the car rockin' for 30 minutes when all of a sudden, the tape flipped. I heard the claps and 808's for the next song coming in, but it was too late to do anything. *Oh, snap...*

"Heeey, we want some pusssaay.
Everybody say... Heyyy, we want some
pussaaay."

"Whaaat!" My mom swerved on the road, then yanked the steering wheel back in place. "What in the hell is that? Is that the kind of stuff you actually listen to?" she asked going through the roof of her car. "I ain't raise you like that." Then, her arm flew across the back seat and popped me in the mouth.

God, I don't wanna die. "I didn't know what was on it," I blurted out. "I got it from my cousin Stick."

I lied too quick. Shoot...it was no sense in getting killed and I hadn't made it back home yet. How the heck could I forget what was on that tape?

I could tell her friend wanted to laugh out loud. He had a smug smirk on his face and I hated it. The look in his eyes said what he wanted to say:

Oh, my, is this the honor roll student she's always bragging on? I knew that little nigga wasn't perfect.

Just like that, the ride began to feel more and more like I was lying in a coffin. I couldn't take it, so I slouched in the corner and imagined Mike Tyson had just knocked me out. That way I could avoid talking about it and let time pass until I saw the sign:

WELCOME TO SAVANNAH

We were finally here and I loved being home. Big porches, fresh seafood, the Talmadge Bridge, historic buildings in the squares downtown, and moss hanging from the trees, were all a part of my city. In 1989, Savannah had three distinct residential areas: the Westside, the Eastside, and the Southside. I lived on the Southside, which for the most part, represented safety, better schools, and a higher economic status.

"Man, the Eastside is different than the Southside," I said looking at a wino hanging in front of a corner store asking for change.

"We ain't long move from out here," Mama said.

"Yeah, I know. I used to love living over here." I reminisced back to the days of playing in Daffin Park and crossing the train tracks on Habersham. "So why do white people mostly live out on the Southside?" I asked.

"You mean why don't they live in the hood?" My mom's friend laughed. "Whites left the inner city during the Civil Rights Movement. I don't think they were too keen on integration. Then, in the late seventies and early eighties, more and more uppity black people seeking a better quality of life moved there as well."

"Uppity?" my mom said a bit offended.

He smiled to lighten the sting. "Well, you know what I mean. Instead of moving out there, black people could have invested in their own neighborhoods."

My mom quickly put her nose in the air. "I don't know about uppity, but I don't want to be 'round folks shooting."

"One side of Victory Drive looks like someone might rob you, while right across the street it looks like white people are swimming in money," I observed.

He was slightly surprised by my comment and turned to look at me. "They're not swimming in money, but I know what you're saying. The good ol' boys have been controlling stuff here a long time."

We pulled up to his house and he got out quickly. He smiled at my mother and waved goodbye like it was romantic in some way. Then he looked at me like he knew that I knew something wasn't right.

On the way across town to our house, we stopped at a red light right in front of the mall. The mall was named after the founder of Savannah, "Old Great James Oglethorpe." All I could think about were the times when my friends and I snuck out of the neighborhood to go there. We would ride each other on the handlebars of our bikes or beg someone to drop us off. The stores and the girls who went there every weekend made it fascinating.

"You wanna stop at the mall?" my mom asked.

"Nah, Ma, you take forever." I laughed. "Every time we go to Belk's it seems like you're holding me hostage. Besides, who wanna go to the mall with their mama?"

She mashed on the brakes in the middle of street. "I was gonna buy you some more stuff for school, but I'll fix you." She hit the gas. "You too cool to go in with me. I'm the same mama who cooks your food and washes your lil' crussy draws."

"Crussy…what kind of word is that?"

"It's a word that best describes those hard brown streaks in your underwear," she sneered before laughing to herself.

It was late in the evening when we arrived, but still muggy outside. I heard the cicadas and swarms of gnats everywhere. When we drove into my neighborhood, my friends, Shawn and Fat were throwing a football up and down the street.

Shawn threw a ball about 20 yards up in the air and it came spiraling down into Fat's hands. Once they saw me, I threw up a peace sign and asked my mom to stop so I could talk.

"Shawn, Fat, what up? Good catch, big man."

"What up, Dez?" Shawn said. "I know you like that arm. I'll teach you how to throw like that one day."

"Is he for real, Fat?"

He stared at me then paused. "Sadly…"

"I'm sorry, let me start again." I put my hands together like I was praying. "Oh, pleeease, Superbowl MVP, show me now."

FLICTED

"Man, forget you," Shawn said, ball in hand. "How was your summer? You get any kisses from them Bama girls or you still half steppin'?"

"Yeah, I met this fine girl at my church."

He couldn't believe it. "Church?"

"Yeah, church, they got girls there, too." I bucked up.

"You ain't 'pose to be thinking 'bout no damn girls at church. You going to hell."

Fat pushed Shawn out of the way. "You got a girl now?"

"Something like that." I rubbed my chin.

"Fat, that means he's lying. Every time he lies his teeth get yellow."

"Man, stop clownin', how was the summer for y'all?"

Shawn threw me a pass. "Cool, Savannah State camp was live as hell. There were so many girls, and it was a bunch of fights. Steve got in it with a couple of fools from the Westside."

"Steve stay throwing hands. 'Sup with Malik and Khalil?" I asked throwing the ball back to him.

"They were gone to Baltimore last week, but they should be home."

"What about them rhymes, though?" Fat asked.

"I been writin' all summer, I got a bunch of new jive."

"I can't wait to hear it. I still remember that freestyle you did last year when I was beat-boxing."

"Oh yeah, that dude, Tori, was at camp acting like he's a rap star. Everywhere we went he was rapping," Shawn added, knowing Tori and I didn't get along. "Matter fact, he almost won the Savannah State talent show."

27

Talent show? I dreamed of being on stage.

Just then, my stepdad pulled up to the driveway. He had one of those big, long, flat boxes of Krispy Kreme donuts in his hand.

"How was your vacation, Derrick?"

"Phil, I had so much fun, I almost didn't come back."

"Don't let your mama hear that." He chuckled. "Fellas, y'all want some donuts?"

Fat immediately jumped in front of Shawn. "You ain't gotta ask me twice."

"We see." Shawn backed up.

"Good to have you back," my stepdad said as I reached for a doughnut. "I need you to help me with the yard tomorrow, alright?"

"No problem. Can we start early before it gets too hot? I'm 'bout to monkey, and it's just in the evening. I can't imagine how hot noon will feel tomorrow."

After kicking it with the fellas awhile, I went inside to grab a couple more donuts and started unpacking. I was so excited for school to start that I laid out all my outfits for the week. I flexed in the mirror for a while and pimped around in the hallway with my new Nike Airs – orange tag included. My head was swelling with conceit. I even tried out a few lame pick-up lines on my pillow to test my game out for the girls.

"Girl, you so fly, it's like you got wings on. When you gon' roll with a red brother like me," I said out loud.

"Red?" my older brother, Rich blurted out, overhearing me as he passed by my room. "Do they call you dirty red or pissy red, cause enquiring minds want to know?"

I threw my pillow at him but he dodged it and continued to talk junk.

"I hope you get a girlfriend this year, so you can stop playing with yourself."

"Whatever, I was just practicing." I was not going to let him ruin my moment.

There were two days until school started and I couldn't wait. If you ever felt it, you know that feeling is everything. Nothing compares to the first day of school.

CHAPTER 3

BUST A MOVE

"This is a jam, for all the fellas. Try to do what those ladies tell us. Get shot down cause you overzealous. Play hard to get and females get jealous."

-Young MC

August 1989

On the first day of school, I sprang out of bed, killed a bowl of Frosted Flakes, and hurried down the street to Shawn's house. The morning air felt like someone had me in a headlock. It was hot and humid. I went to sleep at one o'clock in the morning, yet the allure of the first day gave me the excitement I needed to stay awake. I was a cool, rising eighth grader at one of the brightest schools in town: Westley Wallace Law. Somehow, I knew it would be a year to remember.

FLICTED

Shawn and I were homeboys, though we had gotten into a fight right before the summer. I think I stepped in some dog doo-doo or something and he said, "You better not come close to me with that shit on your shoe." I was like, "How this man gon' tell me what I better not do?" As if I didn't have a glob of doo-doo on my shoe. Nonetheless, I accepted his measly dare and stepped right by him while pretending to touch him with it. When I stepped toward him, he boxed me in my mouth and we started fighting. Nobody said I lost, but they had that look like, "Yeah...he kind of cracked your head, bruh."

"Shoot, at least you got in a few good licks," my homeboy, Fat had said.

Oh, well. We fought and then we were friends the next day. Such is the way it goes with dudes growing up. Today, as Shawn and I approached the bus stop, he talked about how funny he was feeling and that he couldn't wait to check the jive out of someone. We were the worst.

"Checking someone" is a Savannah term for playing the dozens (put downs or "your mama" jokes) and whether you wanted to play or not, you were forced to. Every morning somebody would start. People checked what clothes you had on, how your hair looked, how your mama looked, or anything else they could find to make fun of you.

"Stop hiding all the pound cake, Betty," Shawn shouted as my mom's car passed by our bus stop. Then, he turned to me. "Hey Dez, what big boonkie Betty cooked for dinner last night?"

"Nigga, what *your* mama cook?" I snapped back. "We not even gon' talk 'bout how the edges of her hair be all ate up and that Brillo pad wig she be wearing 'round town."

31

"What you talking 'bout, Dez?" Fat said. "Shawn mama fine." He continued, "Lil' weavy, weavy be looking good." Then he gave his imaginary long hair a twirl.

Shawn frowned up and began to point. "Hey, bruh, don't be talkin' bout my mama."

"Ahh, here we go," everybody moaned.

Now, even if a check hurt, you dare not let on or your so-called friends would go in for the kill. It was verbal abuse at its finest.

Hold up... I'm running my mouth and I haven't properly introduced all the fellas.

At this point in the story you met funny man, Shawn, and Fat, who was laid back until you pissed him off. Next, there were two brothers I hung with named Malik and Khalil, plus the official wild man in the bunch, my homeboy, Steve. There were a few other friends that you'll eventually meet who lived close by, but we were the main six who grew up with each other.

This year, when we boarded the bus, I could hardly contain my emotions as I wondered if I would finally get a girlfriend. I also couldn't help but wonder what everyone else thought about their chances.

"This new Big Daddy Kane is raw," I told my homeboy, Malik, while finding a seat on the bus.

He pulled my head phones back and laughed. "You got it so loud, we can all hear it. Is it better than the first one?"

"Yeah, everything's better... the beats, the raps, and the girls on the cover," I said, while pointing to the tape I held in my hand.

"Hold up, let me see the cover again." Fat snatched it from me.

I quickly thought of a way to set him up. "Hey Fat, you gon' step to anybody this year?"

"Yeah, I got a few people in mind."

"A few people in mind, huh? You got your hand and lotion in mind," Shawn joked.

A little steam pumped out of Fat's ears. "Watch it, funny man."

"He ain't got nobody in mind. Remember when we were looking in that Playboy and that joker started hunching the air and mumbling," Malik reminded us.

Shawn quickly added, "Yeah, he was all on your leg and jive, ain't it?"

"Nah, bruh, that man was on your leg," Malik yelled back.

"Talk about exaggerating...man, y'all running that story in the ground."

"Oh, so you don't remember it happening like that, big boy, huh?" Malik questioned.

"Not like I remember Shawn getting beat down when he grabbed old girl's butt."

"Oooh, I forgot about that," I said, cupping my hand to my mouth. "Man, she chased Shawn all the way home and beat that joker with a vacuum cleaner hose."

"Man, that nigga had looked flicteeed when she hit him," Fat poured it on.

"Nah, Dez the one," Shawn said, to switch the focus off him. "Remember when that girl last year yelled from the front of the bus, that his thing was on hard."

"Do I?" Steve jumped in. "He tried to play it off by boxing himself in the nuts. Talking 'bout if he was on hard, he couldn't do this. Boy, I know that shit hurt."

Everybody hollered out.

"Oh my god, my stomach is killing me." Malik clapped his hands together.

It was 8:00 a.m. when we arrived at school and we had ten minutes to make it to homeroom. I had on an outfit that matched my Nike's down to the stitching and I walked with this serious b-boy bop. I looked at the letter I received with my new homeroom on it; then, I looked for my class. I pimped in through the door and there she was. I flashed back to the note that I found in my magazine. Was it really her?

CHAPTER 4

SHOW 'EM WHATCHA' GOT

*"D-E-Z – yeah, I'm in the
house, live from Westley Wallace,
plan to go to college, from S-A-V- a
dope M.C. hear me E-93/ or MTV."*

**-A Freestyle-under-my-
breath while in homeroom**

"Good morning, Westley Wallace Middle School.
This is your principal, Mrs. McKane and blah blah
blah…"

As the principal finished the announcements, I
wondered who actually listened to all that bull jive. Jive
was a funny word we used in Savannah for almost
everything. It was a magic word that you could use when
you couldn't think of a word to say. We said phrases like,
"What kind of jive is that?" and "Hand me your jive to
pay for it," or even used it as a verb, "This man jive
'round too much."

Anyway, back to this jive. I was busy catching up
with friends in homeroom when I thought about the note,

35

and stared at *her* again. Her name was Kalia Sims. I had a crush on Kalia so hard, I felt a rush of heat sizzling throughout my whole body. That brown gingersnap smile and those gorgeous Janet Jackson dimples made her irresistible. I couldn't talk about her in comparison with other girls. Kalia had a body like a grown woman. I wanted to ask her about the note but the fear of rejection had my lips cemented shut.

Instead, I started to daydream like I had done so many times last year. Within seconds, she sashayed across the class and sat in my lap to talk. Next, she rubbed my head and began to slowly kiss me, until...*dag, the bell! Back to reality.*

Hitting the hallway on the way to first period was chaos. Let me say that again – Chaos. There were people running around, yelling out:

"Tatemville!"

"Liberty City!"

"Westside!"

Some dudes were checking out girls' boonkies, talks of fights were in the air, and lots of people were lost trying to find their way to new classes.

When I came out of homeroom that day, it felt different. It was as if I had some sort of unannounced title now that I was in the eighth grade. I ducked and dodged the mayhem until I saw Malik.

"Boy, the hallways are crazzzy." I looked down to see if my sneakers got scuffed in the crowd. "What you been listening to lately?" I asked.

"My dad just bought me that Public Enemy album."

"Man, your pops is cool as hell." I patted him on the back. "My mom be trippin' when I play music. She always says it's too loud and I know she doesn't understand a damn thing."

"Yeah, my old man is definitely cool...when he wants to be."

Malik's old man was heavily into music and listened to a lot of jazz. He was no joke on the discipline and he always stopped us from saying, "nigga" when we played in their yard.

With that thought and a few minutes before the next class, I gave Malik some dap and moseyed around the corner. Then out of nowhere, a group of girls stepped to me. Most of them were standing around giggling while the leader of the hive, a girl with a pecan tan complexion and the prettiest among them, approached. I had seen her talking with my niece, Nia, a couple times last year, but I didn't know her name.

She walked right into my path so I had to stop. "Hey, Derrick, what's up? I'm Jasmine. You know I want to talk to your fine friend, Malik, right?"

"Know? I don't even *know* you."

She put her hand on her hip as if to say, how dare I not know her name. "Look, I want you to give him my number for me."

"Oh, you like him," I said.

She looked at me like I was dumb as shit, but by this time, I was busy checking out one of her friends.

"He's cute, but he too light for me," the girl I was staring at said, as she pushed by to go to class.

All of a sudden, Jasmine squeezed my arm. "Look, please give him my number." Then she wrote it on a piece of paper and handed it to me. At that moment, the bell rang and I rushed in my first period.

"Hello, don't be late to my class again," my new teacher said.

I saluted him and took a seat.

In history class, I thought about what happened in the hallway. It reaffirmed that 8th grade was going to be different. Then, from my self-induced coma, I heard Mr. Jenks introduce himself.

"Welcome to Georgia History, where you will actually learn, Georgia History," he snickered. "In my class, you will work hard, but you'll enjoy it and have fun. Respect me and I'll respect you, straight up."

Mr. Jenks was speaking our language and you could tell he was cool. History was always my favorite subject, so it seemed like a perfect fit.

After two more classes, the lunch bell finally rang and we left for lunch, then recess on the field. Our school had a big open lot with enough space to play football and run around.

Some people posted up on the wall as if they were posing for *Black Beat* or *Word Up!* magazine. You could tell everyone wanted to be seen.

"Shawn, where's Malik? I met this cute girl that wants to holler at him."

He began to brush his hair for his waves to show.

"You sure she wasn't talking about me?"

"Negro please, yeah, I'm sure." Turning to Fat, I asked, "How were your classes?"

He stretched his arms like he had just gotten out of bed. "Boring... how can your class be boring on the first day? And to think they go to college to learn how to be boring."

Shawn interrupted, "Dez, what are you doing in Ms. Williams' math class? I thought you were in Honors?"

"It's crazy, last year when we took our big tests, I marked anything down."

"Okay, that was dumb," Shawn said.

"Dumb da dumb dumb-duuuuuum," Fat chimed in with sound effects.

"Thanks for the Tums commercial." I played down his joke.

"Well, I guess I can chill since the work'll be easy."

"No, you can't. Ms. Williams looks good, but she don't play. She made me earn my little seventy and she gave a dude in my class a twenty-nine last year," Shawn advised.

We had a few minutes left for lunch, when Shawn nudged me and motioned toward the gym.

A crowd was gathering quickly. "They 'bout to rap, you gon' bust one, Dez?"

"Nah, I'm chilling. I'll go check it out, though."

"Why you chilling?" Shawn shook his head.

Just then, Steve walked up and wanted me to spit, too. "C'mon, ya man, Tori was rapping on the early lunch. What's up."

"So what? That man flow be tired," I said, looking up at the sky.

"Well if you better than him, serve him."

We all headed toward the crowd, while this dude from Tatemville was flowing.

"Where I come from y'all couldn't relate
Don't beef with the best
I play for high stakes.
Westside Savannah
straight from the Ville

Come through talkin junk
you might get killed."

When he finished, Tori jumped in.

"It's Tori, you bore me.
I take the glory
Standing on a building, at the top story.
When I turn forty
I'll still kick flow.
See, suckers stay quiet.
I'm the name you know."

They both traded lines until a female I knew named Angela set it off. I had no idea she could flow.

"Awwh hell, let a female get some.
I snatch mics, then hold 'em for ransom.
Kidnap rap styles and execute it.
I'm what you call fresh.
You boys smell polluted."

"Ohh!" The crowd shouted for more until our teachers crashed the party.

"Everybody clear out now," they yelled. "Go to class, go to class."

"Man, it was just getting good." Fat threw his hands in the air.

I looked away for a second, disappointed in myself for not joining in. "Yeah, I liked the first dude and the girl."

"I think they call him T-Man and you know the girl, that's Lo-lo," Fat said as we walked off.

I wasn't quite ready for the whole school to know that I rapped, but ever since my older brother, Rich, turned me on to hip hop albums like Steady B's *Bring the Beat Back,* and LL's *Bigger and Deffer,* I had become hooked. Whenever class was boring, which was often, I wrote lyrics.

Today after lunch when my English teacher started running his mouth, I wanted to jump out the window. He talked so much about rules and parts of speech; I had to write rhymes to keep my sanity. Finally, the bell rang for the end of the day and the whole class let out one big "Thank you, God."

I threw on my Walkman and bopped over to the bus ramp. I couldn't wait to tell Malik about Jasmine.

The faster I walked, the more my mind fixated on the note with her phone number. "Welcome to the world of women," I thought I'd say to him. Jasmine was a sexy little thing and it was something extraordinary about her.

Nothing could spoil the first day of school. Everything was dope. Or, so I thought. Right after I stepped on the bus, Tori, the rapper, brushed up against me. I looked back and he said something slick. It had a tone that I didn't like and after almost fighting him last year, I wasn't feeling him at all.

I inhaled slowly and thought about punching him when Fat grabbed me by the arm.

"Hey, I heard you 'pose to battle Tori," he whispered to me and Malik.

I looked confused. "Battle? Who… told you that?"

"Your man, Steve."

"Man, Dez can't rap. Every time he rap, he sound like somebody else. Who you gon' rap like today?" Malik laughed.

All the anger I had for Tori was now directed at Malik. *How could my best friend say some foul jive like that?* I was hot. I didn't know how many battles I prepared for in my standing-room-only bathroom, but now I was nervous. *What if they call me wack?* I tried to think of raps that I pieced together over the summer, but it was too late.

"Yeah, what's up, I wanna hear what you got," Tori huffed at me.

"What I got?" I took off my book bag. "Who you, the police?"

Shawn was more than delighted. "Hey Fat, hit them boys with a beat box. Dez been saying he can rap, now I wanna see this."

"I've heard both of 'em rap." Steve followed. "I don't know who gon' win, though."

Without hesitation, Fat made serious drum patterns with his mouth; you could feel the deep bass he belted out when he hit each note. Everybody was locked into him and ready to hear what we had.

"Hold up a damn minute," the driver said, reaching for his walkie-talkie. "Let me call Principal McKane. All y'all better sit down or I'm pulling this bus over."

Fat's beat box kept drowning out the bus driver yelling at us, but even his box was no match for the sound of fear in my heart.

Tori rapped until everybody's mouth was wide open from the stuff he was saying. Then at the height of it, he reared his head back and spit his last line, "Sup, I put yellow boys on a plate / and take a bite / kiss your lil' ass goodnight."

"Ooh." The whole bus was laughing and pointing at me.

I looked at Malik and thought about the phone number in my pocket. I wasn't about to give him shit. When we got off the bus I wanted to duck and hide, but I had to face the angry mob that was ready to let me have it.

"Why you ain't rap?" Fat asked like he was madder than I was.

Steve couldn't believe it. "Dag bruh, you ain't say nothing. Nothing."

"Oh my god," Shawn squeezed out while claiming he couldn't breathe. "That man called you yellow, like fuck all light-skinned people forever. You still feel black after that?"

I sighed hard enough to blow a whole cloud into the air.

Steve walked up from behind, "Nah, Shawn, that jive was a double metaphor, yellow mean that nigga scary."

I looked up briefly, then grinded my teeth. "I ain't scared, I just couldn't think."

"If I were you, I'd battle that dude tomorrow. Ain't no way he could say some shit like that to me," Steve insisted.

Why couldn't I get my words together? It was all in my head, 'til I needed it. *Dag!*

Now, I had to get my respect back. Malik and I had been down since the 5th grade. How long could I really keep from telling him about Jasmine?

CHAPTER 5

RING, RING, RING

*"Hey, how ya'
doin'? Sorry you can't get
through but if you leave your
name and your number, I'll get
back to you."*

-De La Soul

A couple of days later, when I passed Jasmine in the hall, her eyes pierced through my soul. I knew she wanted to know if I had given him the note.

"Nah, not yet," I said, before she could ask.

She was confused by my lack of dedication to the mission and her face conveyed her feelings.

"Dude, you trippin'. You're supposed to be helping me. What's up?"

I felt guilty, so when I got home that Thursday, I picked up the pants I wore on Monday from the floor of my closet. I reached into my pocket and the number that Jasmine gave me fell out. I played back the scene in the hallway on the first day of school and I actually started getting jealous. I mean, dag... she looked good, too. Hmmm...

Then I thought to myself, *Hey, why not give her a call?*

I mean, she liked my man and all... and I wasn't trying to steal her. I just thought I could use her as a way in to her friends, like that cute girl who had jokes in the hallway. Or maybe in truth, I wished it had been me that she chose. I wasn't sure what it was, but something inside stirred me to call.

I picked up the phone, took a deep breath and dialed her number. Mind you, this was the first girl I had talked to on the phone in middle school. So, this was indeed uncharted territory.

When I dialed her number, the phone rang and rang until an answering machine came on. I wasn't sure if I dialed the right number so I waited five minutes or so to call back. I couldn't believe I was calling.

"Hey, who is this?" she said finally answering the phone.

I tried to disguise my voice by lowering the pitch. "It's Malik, what's up?"

Man, she busted out laughing. "This ain't no Malik." Then, she asked, "Dez?"

"Yeah, it's me. I was just messing with you."

"Yeah right, did you give him the number?"

"My bad, I forgot. I know he likes you, though. He kept saying how fine you were when I pointed to you in the hall."

The way she paused after I said it, let me know she really liked him.

"Hey, how do you know my niece, Nia?" I asked to avoid telling another lie about Malik that I might regret.

"Niece." She paused. "How the heck is she your niece when both of y'all are in the same grade?"

I leaned back in my chair to get comfortable, "My older brother, Paul married her mom when we were young."

"Dag, you got a brother that old?"

"Yep, most of them are that old. I came along late, like oops we didn't mean to have him."

"You're funny, Dez." She giggled. "How long have you known Malik? I used to see y'all together in school last year."

"We were in the same fifth grade class and we been cool since then."

It turned out that Jasmine and I knew a lot of the same people even though, unfortunately, we had never directly crossed paths. She was a hip black girl with maturity beyond her age, brimming with charm, sass, and charisma. It almost felt like having a cool younger sister, and she damn near laughed at everything. Even her laugh was funny. It was the type of laugh that when something wasn't that funny, you still laughed at her laugh, if that makes sense.

"Okay, now why don't you have a girlfriend?" she wanted to know.

I can't come across lame, let me think. "I got a girl, but... she goes to another school on the Eastside."

"Oh, I asked 'cause I know a few girls who think you're cute. I'll have to tell them too bad, too sad, then."

When she said that, someone could have dropped a nuclear bomb on my house and I would have been unfazed.

"Like me? H-h-hold up, now. Who, what...you don't know anybody who likes me," I said.

"Yeah, my friends Shanel and Gina both said you were cute and they love how you walk."

Whoa, these were some names me and my friends had talked about.

Next thing you know, I was straight up daydreaming on the phone.

"What's wrong? You act like you don't believe me. Okay, watch this, just be quiet."

"Watch what?" Before I could keep drooling over the names she mentioned, the phone was ringing in a three-way call.

"Hello?"

Man, the voice that said hello back to Jasmine was so heavenly. It seemed like she was from another planet. I heard a slight Savannah street accent in her voice, but it also had a properness to it that was distinct.

"What up, Stank?" she said. Jasmine had called her friend Shanel and started talking to her as if I wasn't there.

"Girl, guess what? I gave Malik's friend my number to give him."

"For real? Who?"

"Girl, his friend, Dez."

"Whaaat?" she exclaimed. I smiled. "Umm, Dez and his lil' cute red self," Shanel added.

What, what! Wait a minute, rewind that thought... and then I played it back in my mind in slow motion: *Dez and hiiis cuuute reeed seeelf...*

Okay, got it.

"I thought he was scared of the poom-poom. I've never seen him talking to girls," Shanel said.

Jasmine howled. "Girl hush, you ain't giving nobody no poom poom."

"Trick, I do the nasty all the time…. Haaa. Bye, my mama calling me to wash the dishes."

"I'll talk to you later."

When they hung up, there was an uncomfortable pause. I didn't know what to say.

Finally, Jasmine killed the silence. "Derrick, I like you, so I'm going to hook you up. Bump your little girlfriend."

"Hook me up? You want me to cheat on my girl?" I asked with my fake deep voice.

"Boy, you crazy, I know you don't have a girlfriend. It's cute how you trying to front."

"Front, me?"

"Yeah, you, boy," Jasmine said. "So, look, I'm going to hook you up, okay? Goodniiight, Deeez."

For me, this was big. No more humping the pillow, no more singing songs in the mirror pretending to kiss someone, and no more lonely death-threatening erections. *A girlfriend?* I couldn't seem desperate; I was at least that hip.

I hung up and drifted off to another world. We had been on the phone for hours and I knew 8th grade would never be the same.

FLICTED

CHAPTER 6

JUVENILES

*"I'm a Menace to Society
juvenile delinquent. Can't stand
school cause I'm in trouble frequent.
Living in the office like it's my class.
See if school's about trouble, maybe
then I'll pass."*

-Poison Clan

The way Friday morning exploded, I forgot to tell Malik about Jasmine. Everyone was talking about a football game we had played last week when Steve noticed Fat's outfit.

"Hey y'all, this man jogging suit FAAAKE." Steve pointed. "His Adidas sign looks like the M in McDonald's," Steve laughed.

Fat looked like an angry sumo wrestler with his arms folded. "Man, my jive ain't fake, and even it was, it's mine. 'Stead a worrying about me, you need to wash your musty ass."

Steve tilted his head while lifting an arm. "Boy, you don't smell nothing but Brut." He turned to the others. "He mad now, y'all."

"Nah, I ain't mad yet, blacky, but you need to stop all that damn playing," Fat pointed.

Steve cracked his knuckles. Blacky? Who your big behind callin' Blacky? I rather be black and fly than big and FAT."

"How, 'bout I'm big and fat enough to kick your ass."

"Say it to my face!" Steve shouted.

They started swinging at each other like it was batting practice. The only ones that got hit was us trying to break them up. Fat was stronger than everybody, which made it difficult to separate them. With that start to my day, everything else was a blur.

I didn't see Malik during school to tell him about Jasmine and after school, I rode the bus to check out my cousin, Marcus. I rode Marcus' bus home with him to a neighborhood named Liberty City and that Friday was bananas.

My cousin Marcus' bus was like my bus on steroids. The checks were way harder and two rival neighborhoods rode the same bus home. This meant that at any moment, World War III could break out. Some folks knew me from school; those I didn't know looked at me when I got on like, "Bruh, who you is?"

That day his bus was super crowded.

"Hey ol' dick in the boonkie ass nigga, move out the way so my cousin can sit down," Marcus said.

"Why I gotta be that?" Marcus' quarry asked.

"Would you rather me call you a faggot?" Marcus barked.

"Man chill, I'll move," the guy said.

On that bus route from school to his house, we shot through Tatemville and then into Liberty City. There was booming music, dope boys hanging on the corner, boarded up homes, and broken down cars along the route.

I also noticed that the females on this side of town had a different sassiness and toughness that you just did not see on the Southside. I loved it. I looked at all of this and interpreted it as 'real life'.

We had gotten off the bus and began to talk about the time I fell off his dirt bike when we passed by a scraggly lookin' dude walking up the block.

Dude had on a coat in August, which was pretty strange.

"Hey Big Marcus, where the sess at?" Dude asked.

Marcus looked at his pager. "Hold up, let me call Reg when I get home."

"Damn, a nigga trynna smoke on somethin' now and ya'll in my way," Dude muttered while walking off.

"What's all that about? And when you get a pager?"

"Nothing cuzo, big boy talk."

I knew how to interpret what I had just seen but I couldn't tell on my cousin.

He changed the subject. "Hey, how was Alabama this summer?"

"Oh. I had too much fun, cuzo. I went to the beach and a place in Panama City called Miracle Strip...it's kinda' like Six Flags. What was going on back here?" I asked.

"I got with so many girls," he whistled. "There were a couple of pool parties and the skating rink... Mannnn, it was jumping all summer."

"The skating rink in Alabama was jumping, too."

My cousin's eyes opened wide. "What the girls look like over there?"

"They're real straight, but its way more girls here in Savannah to choose from."

When we made it to his house, he picked up the basketball laying in the yard and started to dribble before asking me, "You worked on your J over the summer?"

"Yep. Watch this…" I snatched the ball and ran full speed on his court, to stop at the 3 point line. The net on the goal was brand new and ready for some action. I shot the ball.

SWIIISH!

"Awww, that was a lucky-ass shot."

"Lucky…hey, man, how you got titties? You need to run laps or something."

"Here you go trying to be funny with them dragon-ass teeth," he responded.

That check set it off. We wrestled to see who had gotten the strongest since we last met. At first I got the upper hand …only to have him get mad and toss me down to win the match.

From the ground I shook my head and laughed.

"Hey, you know Jasmine and that girl named Shanel?"

"Them stuck up broads? Yeah, I know 'em. They're cute and all," he said, "but they're too stuck up. You won't ever get any from them."

He kind of made me feel bad for mentioning them, 'til I thought about it. "Oh, what you meant to say is *you* wouldn't get none, right?"

He grinned. "Oh, and you would?"

I got up off the ground and drew a silhouette of them in the air with my hands, "Shanel is fine, bruh," I rebutted. "She got that pretty dark skin. Somebody said she's half Dominican, but I don't know what that means."

"Whatever, we be calling her MC Chin. She ain't all that."

"MC Chin?" Maybe I missed something.

"Yeah, she got a long-ass cartoon character chin."

"Ah, you trippin,'" I waved. "I don't care what you say. I know fine when I see it."

Marcus was always a bit rougher around the edges and more street than I was. So when he called the girls I mentioned stuck up, I knew where he was coming from. He once told me how he had sex while he was in the 5th grade while I sat in amazement.

"You did what? With who? And it felt like what?" I had asked.

As crazy as some people thought my cousin was, to be honest, I was very thankful for him. It helped my reputation around school to have a cousin who was ready to throw hands, and I was cool with a lot of dudes that I probably would not have been cool with if not for him.

"Hey Dez, listen to this. Y'all southside boys don't know 'bout this."

"Whatever," I said, letting out a big yawn in disapproval.

"You ever heard of Jam Pony DJs?" he asked.

"Man, they sound like a bunch of drunk uncles, why are they rapping over the songs?"

"You never heard of Poison Clan either, have you?"

"Are they fresh?"

"Check this song out, it's called *Juveniles*."

My cousin bopped to the beat as I listened. In the song, one of the rappers talked about beating the shit out of his dad since his dad beat him the last time he got all F's. This was definitely different from Public Enemy. It was funny and it reminded me of lyrics N.W.A. would spit, but with a southern accent.

Nonetheless, I dozed off thinking of how fun it would be to live in Liberty City. Little did I know, that day would come soon, along with a whole lot of conflict. Especially, when I found out what my cousin was really into.

CHAPTER 7

IT TAKES TWO

Ladies like me, girls adore me.
I mean even the ones who never
saw me, like the way that I rhyme
at a show. The reason why? Man, I
don't know. So let's go, cause…"

-Rob Base & DJ E-Z Rock

"Oh snap, bruh, I forgot. Guess who like you…" I asked Malik at the bus stop on Monday.

"Bruh, you late. Jasmine gave me a note on Friday. I've been talking to her over the weekend. She told me y'all talked, and she thinks your lame butt is kind of cool."

"Yeah, yeah, look at you," I said while giving him a light punch on the shoulder.

"I'm going to walk to her house on Wednesday. Why don't you walk with me? She said her friend Gina might be 'round there."

Now, I didn't know too much about Gina, but it seemed like a trip I couldn't dare pass up.

That day, school was uneventful, but Wednesday afternoon came like lightning. I was on the bus, rapping the lyrics to *Straight Out the Jungle* with Steve, when this cute Jamaican girl on our bus chimed in, **"Cool and quiet, but quick to start up a riot / I write the rhymes, bums insist to bite it."** Then, she paused for a second. "That's my song, right there," she said as she did the Cabbage Patch dance.

At that moment, Steve jumped up, did this crazy crack head jig like Flavor Flav and we all laughed. Well, everyone except for Malik.

"Dag, c'mon, bruh, 'least ask me first."

"At least ask me," I said mocking him.

"You still walking to Jasmine's house?"

"I don't know." He turned his back toward me. "I may need to leave you, since you're snatching food."

"Sure, you do. It seems like she stays close to Jay and Head."

He put the rest of his chips in his pocket. "Yeah, that's what it sounds like from what she said. Be at my house at four thirty and we'll walk."

"Bet."

On the way to Jasmine's house, I felt like a man. We weren't going to see my girl, but my chest was poking way out. "I know you don't think you about to get no loving." I elbowed Malik to mess with him.

"You just salty cause we're going to my girl house."

"Your girl?" I asked.

"That's what I said."

When we arrived, Jasmine came to the door looking fine as a mug. Her friend, Gina didn't come and since our homeboys, Jay and Head, lived close by, I walked there to give the lovebirds some privacy.

Everybody in my neighborhood was cool with Head and his older brother Jay. They used to live closer but had moved deep into the Southside of town the year before. Jay was hip and had this 'I'm from New York thing' going. He was born there and every summer when he came back from visiting, he would have all the latest styles: Dwayne Wayne Flip-up Glasses, Nike Mountain Boots, and he was the first person I knew who walked around school with a briefcase.

Head was different. He was real laid back and a certified hooper. He loved basketball and thought he was the next Tim Hardaway in the making. His real name was Montez, but we all called him Head since he had a pretty big one.

"What them handles look like, Head?" I asked, swiping at the ball he was dribbling.

"Dez, you can't guard me. You better stick to rapping."

"Ahhh. What's up? Last time you were at Chatham Gardens, we put it on you," I bragged.

"Boy, you stay exaggerating. Y'all beat us with a lucky shot at the end of the game. Whenever you ready, let me know."

While Head kept dribbling, Jay finally came outside.

"What were you doing?" I asked.

"Oh, finishing up some homework. You know how young black engineers do it." Then he swiped the ball from Head. "Hey, Dez, Malik told me that girl Jasmine likes him. I see your boy done came up."

"I know, right. But hold up, Jay, where *your* girl at?" I put my hand up to my ear.

"Right next to your girl," he shot back.

"Man, you know my girl live on the Eastside, bruh,"

"Yeah, yeah, lies. What's going on? Malik told me Steve and Fat almost got into it again."

"Yeah, they was 'bout to fight 'til we broke it up. Other than that, we been messing with Shawn about the rubber incident."

"Rubber incident?" Jay asked.

"Man, this jive here funny. Okay Steve was checking Shawn the other day, right? He said that while he was in the store, Shawn asked the clerk for some rubbers."

"Who letting Shawn get down like that?" Head interrupted.

"Well, that's just it. When Steve asked Shawn, 'Who you need rubbers for?' this fool said Shawn hollered 'bout he wear them jives in case he have a wet dream."

"A wet dream?" Jay snickered. "No, it ain't—I don't believe that." Jay laughed.

"Man, I ain't lying. He had us 'bout to lose it," I said.

"I mean, we all have 'em, but I'm not putting on no rubber just in case. That's crazy as hell," Jay said.

"Don't act like you ain't ever done it, Dez." Head laughed.

"To be honest, the first time it happened, I didn't really know what was going on. I woke up and thought I peed in the bed 'til I felt how sticky it was. I thought my jive was broke or something. Then I asked my stepdad and he explained. I was relieved as hell."

"Dez, you crazy, bruh," Jay said while stomping his foot.

I tripped out with them for another hour to give Malik time before I called. "You ready?" I asked.

"I will be by the time you get here."

On the way back, he kept smiling.

"Man, that girl is sillaaay."

"Silly how?" I wanted to know.

He paused and looked to the sky like he was thinking of a way to say it but couldn't. "Hey, what you think about Jasmine?"

"I think she a keeper. And she real cool, bruh."

"Yeah, I think so, too. That's why I asked her to go with me."

"Whaaat." I backed up to give him space.

When he said that, I looked at Malik in a whole new light. He and his manhood had arrived.

"How did you ask?"

"Hey, Big Brother Almigh-T doesn't share details." He smirked.

I stopped walking and just looked at him. "Don't act like this isn't your first girl in a hot minute."

"Look," he started. "She already said she liked me. It was easy. She tapped my shoulder a few times and looked the other way pretending to be shy. So, I grabbed her hand and kissed those sexy ass lips of hers. Then, she kissed me back and bruh, we went at it. Shoot after that, I asked her to go with me."

The way he described it, I felt like I was there. I tried hard not to be jealous but I was.

After we made it to his house, I ran down the street to make it home until I bumped into Fat. He was outside, finishing yard work with his grandfather.

The lawnmower was on so I put my hands together like a bullhorn, "Faaat."

He stopped and turned around. "What up, Dez? Why you cheesin' so hard?"

"What up, yard Man? I just walked with Malik to see his new girl, Jasmine."

"What he take *you* for, then? Some kind of protection?" He laughed.

"I'm cool with her too, plus one of her friends was 'pose to be there. She didn't come, but you know Gina, right?"

"Ugly-in-the-face-but-got-a-boonkie, Gina?"

"Nah, not that Gina. Bow-legged Gina."

"Oh, that Gina is fine. So, it's Malik and Jasmine now, guess he big time, huh?" Fat asked.

"I guess. Shoot, we all need to be big time, if you ask me."

His grandfather was yelling at him to hurry up and finish, so I said, "Later," and walked on home. I was feeling better and actually proud of Malik, but it was time to get a girl of my own.

CHAPTER 8

THE GREATEST MAN ALIVE

> *"Hittin' with the hardest,*
> *coming with the clarity. Skying*
> *over suckers, defying laws of*
> *gravity. The style of my hair like a*
> *new wave Afro. EST's the unusual*
> *fellow."*

-Three Times Dope

September 1989

By the time I hit 13 I had been to Las Vegas, Key West, Greece, and New York. This was all courtesy of my Nintendo and one of my favorite games, *Rad Racer.* Even though I was into my game, all I thought about was improving my chances of getting girls. *Maybe I should dye my hair or get a part on the side? Nah, my mom would never go for that.* I had just reached the next level on my game when the front door opened and slammed.

"Derriiick!" my mom yelled out. She entered my room and balled up her face at the explosion of junk. "I'm fixin' to go to your granny house. Get your shoes and ride with me."

"Okay, can I finish my game?"

"Look, I need to go. Come on now or you can stay and clean this mess up."

I moved quicker than lightning. When I got inside, she was humming some sort of tune. I couldn't make out the song, but every time she hummed or sang, it reminded me of opera music. By the way, I hated opera music.

"How school going?" She looked at me like it better be going good.

"Everything's straight, especially in math," I said, as we drove down Augusta Avenue.

My grandmother lived in West Savannah, and at the time I didn't really like going there unless it was for the holidays. This part of town was filled with lots of churches, tight narrow streets, and families who had known each other for years. It was an older part of town that seemed boring since it didn't have big stores and a mall like the Southside. And my grandmother always made me get her 'bacca cup, which was an old tin can full of thick, dark, sticky spit that made me nauseous anytime I had to look at it.

Whenever I went there, I had flashbacks of an incident that happened when I was about five. My mom had just whooped me good for something and I wouldn't stop pouting about it. Frustrated, she threatened to give me another whooping, 'til my grandma stepped in.

"Boy, hush. You're too big to be doing all that crying. Now if you a baby, then Granny gon' give you some titty milk."

I was like, titty what? Man, I swear she whipped her jive out and pushed it up against my head to stop me from crying. It was all flabby and wrinkled up. Yeah, I got quiet all right, albeit traumatized at the same damn time. I had to have looked like I was about to vomit.

Anyway, we made our way through the front gate and she was in the kitchen cleaning up when we arrived.

"Hey Betty, who that little white boy walking behind you?"

"Dez, you hear what Mama call you?" my mom asked.

"Yeah, I heard her. I was unamused. Hey Granny, you have any Thrills made?"

"Only if you hug my neck, you know ol' Granny was just messing with you." She smiled.

Thrills were these little frozen cups of juice with a popsicle stick in them, that people made and sold from their houses. It was a West Savannah trademark, and my grandmother made some of the best.

I was sitting at the table sucking on one, when my cousin, Shareef, came up on the porch.

He was one of the coolest people I knew. He had introduced me to Eric B. and Rakim back when my age group was still listening to Run DMC. At first, I didn't like it, but once I caught the feel of *Paid in Full*, I knew it was incredible.

"Y'all gon' stop talking bad 'bout Atlanta," Shareef shouted at a dude outside.

"Man, the Falcons ain't nothing but a disappointment." the dude shouted back.

"I'm telling you that boy, Deion Sanders is raw, watch and see."

"But that's just one player. They need 21 more Deions."

"Alright, alright, later…"

Opening the door, he took his hat off and greeted everyone before going over to kiss my grandmother.

"Hey there, lil' cuz, what it is now? You playing for the sorry Southside Raiders this year or you ready for a real team like the Whippers?" Both of these were Pop Warner teams in our area.

Before I could respond, he called out, "Aunt Betty, you mind if Dez rides to Atlanta with me this weekend? I'm going to see Evette," he added.

"How's my niece doing?"

"She good, Auntie, I talked to her last night."

"How long are you staying?" my mother wanted to know as she looked up from her plate of food.

"Til Sunday morning."

"All right that's fine, just take care of my baby."

"Baby?" Shareef chuckled. "I forgot you were a mama's boy."

"Man, go head on with that mama's boy shit," I said under my breath.

Now that I could go to Atlanta, I was ecstatic.

At lunch the next day, instead of sitting down next to Jay and Malik, I sat on the table. "Hey y'all, I'm 'bout to ride to Atlanta with my cousin on Friday. This man gets all kind of girls. He got a fresh ride, too."

"Well, get him to get you a girlfriend, then," Malik suggested.

Jay's eyes sparkled. "Your cousin doing it like that?"

"Malik, why you trying to dis me on the sly?"

He opened his milk carton and took a sip. "Dis you? You the one bragging, I just thought I would be helpful and point out the obvious. Besides, you gotta step to girls and not just talk about them."

Jay laughed so I tossed my bread roll at Malik and started walking off. "Alright, I will ask him to get me one. Thanks, punk."

"You do that." Malik looked over at Jay. "Or you can bust one of your little raps, that'll get the girls for sure."

"Boy, you and Dez are funny," Jay interrupted. "I thought y'all were homies?"

Malik grinned. "Yeah, that's my man, he's just funny when it comes to girls."

On Friday, Shareef came and picked me up after school in his Toyota Celica. It had just been washed and he had a new pair of chrome rims on it. I walked up to the car like I was getting into a black stretch limo. I wanted everyone to see me. As cool as I could, and as slowly as I could, I carefully placed my stuff in the trunk.

My cousin was ready to go, so he revved the engine a few times and pulled off while making the tires screech.

"Dez, you got any new tapes with you?"

"I got Kid 'n Play in my Walkman."

"You like that shit?" he asked in a mocking voice. "Yeah, I forgot, you young bucks like that bubblegum jive."

"Man, how you gon' play me? I know about all kinds of rap, but I like dancing and "Gittin' Funky" be jamming."

"Well, we ain't playing Kid 'n Play up in here. Put that D.O.C. tape right there, in."

When we made it to Atlanta, we got off on Washington Road at my cousin Evette's nail salon in College Park.

"Is Evette rich?"

"Why you say that?"

"Well she got her own business and that BMW she drives is too fresh. Last time she came to Savannah, I didn't want to get out of it. It's got Gold BBS rims on it and everything."

Shareef poked out his top lip and brushed his mustache with his fingers, "You know 'Vette a hustler. She works hard and plus her old man got bread too."

When we strutted through the salon door, Evette jumped out of her chair to give us a hug.

"Hey, y'all, these are my two cousins, Shareef and my baby cousin, Derrick."

"Hey, baby cousin," a chorus of women echoed the welcome.

"Hey cuz, we're hungry after being on that road." Shareef rubbed his stomach. "We'll head to the mall and come right back."

Greenbriar Mall looked like paradise and there were girls everywhere. My eyes shot out of my head, ran around the block and came back twice. Shareef saw me gawking at just about everything moving.

"Nah, you ain't ready for nothin' like that, young buck. And don't look so thirsty when you check out girls."

"Thirsty?"

"Yeah, you look wild, like your mama had you caged up in the back yard. You gotta look at girls and be cool and smooth about it."

"Whatever. I'm trying to see what I can see, while I got a chance."

He put his hand on my shoulder. "Then look here, and listen to me good…you in for a looong road, lil' cuz."

Once we were done eating, we stopped at a spot called Record Bar.

"Hey, you ever heard of a group called Poor Righteous Teachers from outta Jersey?" he asked the guy up front.

"Not sure. Look in the new releases."

Shareef was hip to a lot of Five Percent Nation teachings. This was a small sect of Muslims who practiced a style of Islam similar to Malcolm X when he was with the Nation of Islam. It was different than regular Islam and it talked about black men being Gods. I believed he picked this up from spending summers in Jersey. 'Cause in the South, you wouldn't hear about Islam as much. These teachings and philosophies influenced his choice of hip hop a lot.

"I haven't heard of Poor Righteous Teachers," I said to him as we made our way to the new releases.

"I'll turn you on, they be droppin' that science."

"Science? That's what Rakim and KRS be saying."

"Yeah, Science is knowledge and knowledge is power, and black people need some power."

"Okay, I gotcha."

Most hip-hop was purely fun, but when you could do both, make fresh songs and drop science, it made the music even more meaningful.

The next day after we toured the city, Evette took us by a friend's beauty shop to introduce us. She looked like Holly Robinson from *21 Jump Street* and her personality bubbled with excitement.

"Hey girl, when you gon' give me them heels?" Evette asked.

She lifted up one of her legs. "You want me to take 'em off now?"

"You ain't 'bout to give me those, so just hush." My cousin laughed. "Girl, his hair looks good."

"Yeah, I stay making everybody look good but me," her friend said, pretending to be sad. "I'm in here so much I don't get time to take care of myself." She was putting the finishes touches on a dude's haircut.

"Girl, you look great, stop playing. Hey, you remember my cousin, Shareef, right?" Evette asked.

"Yeah, I remember him. Hey, Mister Man," she said.

Shareef smiled so big I could see his wisdom teeth. Then he looked at her with one eyebrow raised as if to say, *"I'll holler at you later."* While they joked and gave each other googly eyes, I was in awe of the person sitting in her chair. Once I imagined myself struttin' around school with a new style like that, I knew I had to have it.

"Shareef, you think she'll dye my hair? I want to get it dyed in the front."

"I mean, if that's what you want, lil' cuz. Now hold up— your mama not gon' kill you for getting it done, is she?"

"Nah," which is what I hoped, but I also figured if my new style went over bad, I could blame him for telling me it was okay.

"How much will it cost to dye it?" I asked as if I had money.

"Baby, don't worry, if you Vette's cousin, you my cousin. Ain't no charge."

When I sat down in the chair, I felt like I was close to a moment of greatness. She faded my sides, then stepped back and paused.

"You know, you would look tight with a Gumby."

It had never crossed my mind, but maybe she was right. A Gumby was a flat top that was tilted all the way to the side like the head of the popular cartoon from the 1970s. I thought the style was fresh and I liked the Gumby that a rapper from Philadelphia named EST had, so I did it.

I was too psyched up at that point. I was all in the mirror like I dropped a video on *Rap City*. I kept touching and patting every strand of hair on my head. After my tenth time looking at it, my cousin gave me a bottle of something called Sun In and said I could use it once the dye faded. I couldn't wait to get home.

Unfortunately, when I walked through the door, my mom went slap off. "Lord, you and these crazy-behind haircuts. Now you know I should make you cut that mess off. You want to go to church looking like a wholum."

"Mama, you trying to say hoodlum? This is just a new style, relax."

"Wholum, hoodlum same damn difference. I don't like it. You look like a skunk with that blonde streak in your hair." Finally, she stopped fussing and walked away.

At school, everybody noticed. My sixth sense could feel it when I hit the hall way and then I saw my homeboy, Montez "Head."

"Yo, Dez, that's fresh. Where you get it dyed at?" he asked stepping back to see it from all kinds of angles.

"I was in Atlanta last weekend. I got this dye. I paused and opened my book bag. "If you want, I can spray it on you in the bathroom real quick."

"Yo, it's not going to burn my jive out, will it?" he asked touching his hair.

"Nah, don't worry, I did Shawn's hair earlier. It doesn't turn instantly though, you have to stand in the sunlight to make it change."

Later in the day after hooking Head up, I saw Jasmine on the way to my last class.

"Uh oh, look at Dez, y'all," she shouted.

A few of them were jocking me, so I rubbed my chin and backed against the wall to soak in their admiration.

"You really like it?"

She patted the top of my new cut. "Yeah, it looks sooo cute on you."

Talk about an ego boost. By the time I boarded the bus that afternoon, you couldn't tell me I wasn't a superstar. Now, I had to figure out: *how to use my newfound fame?* Since it was a few days before my birthday, I looked out the window and made a wish. Of course, I didn't really believe in wishes. It was just a fun way to look at things but I hoped…it would come true.

FLICTED

CHAPTER 9

I GOT IT MADE

*"I'm kind of young but my
tongue speaks maturity.
I'm not a child, I don't need
nothing but security. I get paid
when the record's played, to put it
short... I got it made."*

-Special Ed

Late September 1989

Turning fourteen wasn't just any number; I was now poised to become a man. In and outside of my scrawny 100-pound body, I was going through crazy changes. First of all, my voice would start off deep, then crack into Michael Jackson tones without warning. Pimples periodically invaded my nose and I couldn't muster any hair on my face. So, one night I got this dumb-ass idea to cut a few strands from an undisclosed place to glue on my chin. *Yep that's what I need. If I had a little hair, girls would be all over me.*

I moved this peculiar patch of hair around my face to see how it would look. However, I knew it was no way I

71

could pull it off and become Teen Wolf overnight. They say slow and steady wins the race and with my new haircut, I believed my time would come.

Gone were the days of cake and presents. For my birthday, all I wanted was some dead presidents. My parents gave me forty dollars, but I didn't have enough to buy the video game I wanted, so I planned to buy a shirt instead.

We arrived at the mall early Saturday morning after I begged my mom to take me. "Well, where do you want to go? JCPenney's has nice shirts," she said.

I was too insulted. "Mama, nobody wears clothes from JCPenney's but old folks.

I pointed down the hall. "I wanna go to the Stagge Shoppe."

"The where?" She put her hand on her hip.

I pointed again. "That's the place where Rich buys all his clothes.

She nodded reluctantly as we walked inside.

"Now, this is the kind of jive I like," I announced, holding up a blue and orange Polo shirt.

My mom took a quick glance at the ticket, and shouted, "One hundred dollars for a shirt? Man, let me get out of here quick." She shook her head in disgust. "Only your brother would spend that kind of money. He's a fool, you hear me? I asked him to help with a bill the other day and he claimed he was broke. Yet he has money to buy all kind of clothes from up in here?" Mama fussed.

I knew she wanted to tell my brother all about himself, because she went on and on for another five minutes, and the more she talked, the more I laughed. To me though, my brother was the certified Black Ralph

Lauren and with plenty of *GQ* magazines around the house, he indoctrinated me into his world of fashion.

"Why spend so much on a shirt, though?" I asked him once.

He replied, "Look, lil' bruh. Rather than have ten twenty-dollar chump shirts, buy three one-hundred-dollar shirts that no one else has and set the standard."

And set the standard I did. Every chance I got, I would reach for one of his shirts and wear it to school like it was mine. I probably could have saved the money like my mom suggested or used it on something else, but I knew this was gonna make girls take notice, so I spent it all.

When my birthday came that Friday, I felt like I was stepping on stage for an award-winning performance. I wore my new Polo and a pair of my brother's black Guess jeans for all my soon-to-be fans. Then I left the house early to catch the bus.

Going to school, I daydreamed all the way to Mr. Jenks's first period class thinking about my cheesy little wish.

While it was my birthday, Mr. Jenks was all business. In fact, his gift to me was a big-ass blackboard full of notes. I just let out one of those long sighs. "Not again."

A friend of mine in class named Brian had also had enough. "Man, this ol' peanut-head joker is making us work too hard."

"Uh oh, that man heard you, bruh," I whispered.

"Work too hard?" Mr. Jenks said. "Look, it won't help your grade; it's already too low."

"You trying to say I'm dumb, Mr. Jenks?"

"Absolutely not, I'd never do that. But I think your mama said you were the last time I called."

"Oooh!" everyone in class shouted.

"Man...so? Your head still big as hell, bruh."

"Oh, my bad, my head is blocking your education. Let me move so you can show us how smart you really are," Mr. Jenks said.

When he felt like it, he cracked on us with some good ones. This kept the class in control and put people in check quick.

The rest of the day was cool until I saw Steve talking to Shawn at lunch.

"Hey, y'all, you know it's Dez's birthday, time for them licks, bruh," Steve yelled out.

Licks—or punches, in this case—were given to a person by each of their friends based on how old you were and today my lucky number was 14. Since I participated in this rich tradition with others, I knew exactly what time it was.

I ducked and dodged them while we were at school until they eventually caught me getting off the bus. Everybody was crackin' their knuckles and lookin' at me like they couldn't wait. Well, I wasn't gonna sit and just take it, so I got off the bus and tried to make a run for it.

"Man, Steve *catmanned* the shit out of Dez," Shawn shouted.

When he tripped me, I fell on my face real awkward and hard; sort of like Charlie Brown with a cloud of dust over my head.

"You straight?" Steve asked like he was halfway sorry.

FLICTED

"Bruh, what the hell? Okay. Y'all jokers got birthdays too," I said while grabbing Steve to yank him down.

Before I could think of another way to escape, those fools jumped on me laughing and punching 'til I was exhausted. By the time I caught my breath, everybody had run home laughin' and I was forced to take it like a man. Oh, well, what can I say? It was all a part of becoming 14.

When I stepped in my house, Rich was singing along with the music he was playing. I opened up his bedroom door, and walked in.

"Damn, Dez, you ever heard of knocking?"

His girlfriend jumped up off the bed and began to adjust her clothes.

My eyes opened like curtains for the morning sun. "Oh, my bad." Then he shoved me back into the hallway.

"What happened to you?" He examined my injuries. "Damn, you let somebody beat you up?"

"Man, ain't nobody 'round here can beat me up."

"Yeah, right, and you look like they can't," he said, laughing. "Nigga, your jeans got grass stains all in 'em. Look like somebody drug you 'round by your head. Hey... hold up, man, them my damn jeans."

Without waiting for him to finish, I ran to my room and locked the door. My body was still sore from the birthday ritual and I wasn't about to take another lick. He banged on my door like he had a warrant, but I drowned him out with music.

"You know I'ma kill you, right?" he repeated several times before walking off.

After five minutes or so I heard the front door open and shut. Once I knew it was safe. I came out, put his now-dirty jeans under his bed and grabbed the Kool G. Rap cassette that was lying on his dresser. I had been waiting to hear it since I saw the video for his song, "Road to the Riches."

G Rap's rhymes were insane. He bounced words around like Michael Jordan dribbling for a last-second shot. His style inspired me to write tons of raps and realize how serious I had to be to make it.

The next day after school, Steve and I were walking back from the store freestyling when a new dude in our neighborhood named Jarvis rode up on his bike.

"Bruh, how are you gon' come around the corner rapping with tassels hanging off your handlebars on a big-ass banana-seat bike? That ain't hard," Steve joked.

"My bad, *Stevie-E*, stop jocking my style. Anyway, this is my lil' sister's bike."

Jarvis was taller than us and in tip-top shape. He could have easily been a star athlete, but his thing was music.

"Didn't you used to play football for Omar?" Steve asked.

"Yeah, I might play next year, after my album comes out."

"Your album? Boy, please." Steve laughed. "You need to play basketball or football with all that height."

Jarvis acted like he was dribbling a ball with his feet. "That's cool, but I actually might play soccer."

Steve's face turned sour. "Nah, that's a white boy sport."

"White boy? I used to play soccer, too," I said.

"Like I said, white boy sport. You know Dez ass 'bout white," Steve joked.

"Excuse me, Count Blackula," I shot back.

FLICTED

"Both of y'all are retarded. I've never met anybody who checks as much as y'all," Jarvis said as if he was much more mature. Then he bopped around like he was on stage with a microphone in his hand. "What's up, Dez, I heard you be battling dudes at school, I want to see what you got."

I looked over at Steve and he had a funny look on his face like he was guilty. I didn't think Jarvis was that good so I immediately said, "What's up?"

Now that the challenge was official, Jarvis began.

"Alright check it
J-A-R-V-I-S
name me fresh.
Mama said be the best.
I'm a genius above the rest.
I said it.
Talk a foot in ya ass is where ya headed.
Dudes love the style.
Chicks love the smile.
Got too many flows.
You should read my file.
Psycho, rap insane, number one.
My words, just bullets for the gun on my
tongue."

Steve and I looked at each other in amazement. Jarvis was raw and I had to think of a fresh comeback quick. When I had it, my right eyebrow raised. Then I paused for a moment to build anticipation.

"Hold up," Steve looked at me. "What happened to the battle, Dez, don't tell me you scared?"

Jarvis grinned, then tapped me in the chest like he had already won. "We don't have to battle or nothing, I just wanna hear if you can rap."

"I can do a lil' something."

Jarvis laughed. "Alright then, whatchu got?"

> *"I ain't a clown.*
> *I get down for mine.*
> *Keep up and count.*
> *I got a thousand rhymes.*
> *Take a thousand times, never gain an inch.*
> *Wonder who Dez is?*
> *I can tell you tense.*
> *Me, lightweight?*
> *Man I topped the class.*
> *You test the wrong one.*
> *Look, I already passed.*
> *If you ask for a battle,*
> *this is what you get.*
> *Take a good long whiff...*
> *cause I been the shit."*

"Ohhh," Steve shouted and dapped me up. "I knew you had it in you."

Jarvis slightly folded his arms and stared at me. Then, he got hyper than before we started. "Bruh, we gotta do a song together—it'll be crazy,"

"Together, you have a way to record?" I asked.

"Yeah, I got a double cassette radio and a bunch of beats looped up."

Jarvis seemed to know a lot. He was the first person I met who talked about music like I did, but with fire in his eyes.

"Dez, you should be getting all kinds of girls with flow like that, you know how many girls I have on my tip?"

"You know I could manage y'all boys," Steve jumped in again. "You gon' need somebody to take care of the money and stuff."

"Here you go." I looked at Steve sideways.

"Whatever. You know rappers aren't smart enough to write and count...or handle women."

Jarvis could barely move his lips. "What...?"

That night, I went home and wrote inspired for hours. I started hearing these voices in my head that said, *"One day you're going to be great. Just don't stop."*

To be a part of hip hop motivated me more than anything. I felt destined to be an M.C. and have a girl of my own. I still didn't know how to make it happen, but I was ready to go for it all.

CHAPTER 10

EVERY LITTLE STEP

"As a matter of fact, it blows my mind
that you would even talk to me.
Because a girl like you, is a dream come true
a real-life fantasy."

-Bobby Brown

November 1989

The summer was officially long gone, and everybody had started wearing their new starter jackets to deal with the chill. Fall was here and the Coastal Empire Fair was in town. Back then, there wasn't a whole lot to do in Savannah for young teens, so you can imagine how big of a deal a fair was. New rides and a chance to check out girls was all I could think of. I had gone to the fair every year for as long as I could remember, but this year, neither my mom nor stepdad had time to take me. Luckily, Malik called the Friday before the fair left town.

"Hey Dez, if you wanna go, we're leaving at seven."

"Do I wanna go? Bruh, I'll be to your house at six."

On the way to the fair, we checked up a storm in the back seat of Malik's mom's car.

The radio was on and we all knew how to read lips while we joked.

The only thing his mother could hear while she drove was our laughter.

"Shawn, you know all Jasmine has to do is snap her fingers and Malik come running," I teased. "She got that man on a leash."

"Look a' here, bucky boy, chill out before I call Ms. Betty," he said, slightly pissed. "Matter fact, you need a girl, so you can get off my nuts, bruh."

I couldn't let him get the best of me, so I went into my bag of heavy artillery.

"Hey Shawn, Malik mama fiiiine."

As you could imagine, Malik and Khalil never liked it when we did that, but the rest of us got a kick out of it. Plus, their mother was younger than everyone else's and she looked kind of good.

"You just gon' let that man check out your mama boonkie, bruh?" Shawn whispered.

"Man, I ain't checkin' out his mama boonkie. I said she fine; don't let him boost your head up."

"Hey Khalil, these boys don't wanna make it to the fair, they want us to kill 'em in the back seat."

Then we all started laughing.

Any old way, when their mom dropped us off, we bought our tickets, and decided to get in line for the bumper boat ride.

"Malik, y'all rode these before?" Shawn asked.

"Nah, you?"

"Bumper cars, bumper boats, hey, why not?"

"Alright it's your call." Khalil laughed.

We were in a huge pool floating in about five feet of water, driving around in boats like crazy. When the ride was finished, I tried to hop out all quick, and messed around and slipped. I reached out to catch the ledge and save myself but *nope*. I fell right back into the water.

"What was that?" Khalil turned around after the huge splash and then went berserk.

"Hey, y'all, this fool Dez done fell."

Not only was I wet, but it was cold as hell that night and they didn't make it easy to live it down. In fairness, if it happened to one of them, I would have done the same thing. They called me "ol' soggy draws" for about an hour. Eventually, I had to give in and laugh at myself.

"Hey, Dez, you want me to call my mama to pick us up?" Khalil asked.

"Pick us up? Hell nah... we just got here," Shawn insisted.

I was shivering. "Nah, I ain't trying to ruin the night for everybody. I'm straight."

"Yeah, you need to suck that up. Hey, you know what, if we ride the Himalaya, it'll help dry you off," Shawn said.

We ended up riding it three times, and even though my draws were still wet, I did feel a little drier.

Afterwards, we walked around until we bumped into a girl from school named Mya.

She was the type of girl who was cool with everybody.

"Hey, what's up, look at all my handsome friends," she said to the girls she was with. All of us couldn't help but smile.

"Look, I need one of y'all to win a bear for me. I'm tired of losing my money out here." She held up about three dollars. "This is all I have left, help a sister out."

"I got you, Mya." Khalil stepped up and put his arm around her shoulders.

"That's so sweet, don't forget," she said, after giving him a hug.

Shawn waved at the other girls. "Hi, I'm one of the most available young men at the fair tonight." They both looked around and laughed. "And, this...is my wet friend, Dez."

I knew he couldn't keep his big mouth closed. "Oooh, I gotcha ass, bruh," I said while thinking of some serious payback.

Mya came over and touched my shirt. "So Dez, how did you get wet?"

I threw my hands up to playfully laugh at myself and take some of sting out of the situation. "Yeah..." I started real slow and easy. "I kind of slipped in the pool trying to get out of the bumper boats."

Of course, they all died laughing, but one of the girls seemed to feel a bit sorry for me. When we caught eyes, she gave this quick look of concern that I picked up on. *Hmmm...* Afterwards, we all said good night, and they walked away.

Khalil put his hand over his eyes to block the glare from the lights and get one last look. "That red girl was cute."

Shawn shook his head. "Yeah she was in my gym class last year, her name is Briana."

"Yeah, she looked nice," I added while wringing out the last bit of water from my clothes.

That night after the fair, I was beat. I took a shower and went to sleep thinking about all the girls I saw, especially Mya's friend, Briana. *Maybe she was the one.*

****

A few days later, I was chillin' in my room writing a rap to a beat Jarvis had given me when I got a call.

"Hello, who this?" I said real smooth.

Jasmine cut to the chase.

"Dez, first, why you sound like that? Yuck. And what's up with your man? He always wants to get off the phone with me."

"Who, Malik? I don't know, that's just him, I guess."

"He acts like he has a stick up his butt. You need to talk to him. He's starting to make me sick."

And with that she hung up. Jasmine and Malik had one of those love-hate relationships. They would be mad at each other all day in school and then later, act like they were super glued together since birth. I knew they both had things they didn't like about each other, but whatever they were doing or not doing, they kept doing it. My position was to stay out of it.

While she and Malik were growing apart, Jasmine and I continued to become closer. "Deeez," she screamed my name in the hall.

"What up, homey?" I cheesed and gave her a hug.

She backed up and acted as if she was shocked by something. "Why don't you ever write me?"

"What, notes?" I paused.

"Yeah, here, I wrote you one." When I reached for it, she snatched it away, then she smiled before giving it to me right as the bell rang for class.

FLICTED

I didn't know how I should feel. After all, this was my best friend's girl. Still, I loved it.

"What's up, big head?" she started. "My class is sooo boring. My teacher is crazy and this girl in my class breath is stank. She's in here burning up my nose hairs every time she start talking. I'm supposed to be on punishment; no phone for a week. We'll see how that goes. Aren't you glad your best friend wrote you a note?" L/Y/L/A/B p.s. "Stop acting so stuck up."

That day, Fat saw her give me the note, and got inquisitive.

In fact, this fool walked up to me like he had a magnifying glass in his hand. "What Malik girl doing giving you notes? You trying to take that man's girl?"

"Nah, of course not." I played it down. "Jasmine is my homegirl, my magic charm. She has introduced me to all kinds of girls. I'm trying to get her to hook me up."

"Oh, I get it, but does Malik get it. I'd hate to see y'all boys fall out 'bout a girl."

I patted him on his back. "Nah, shit cool, big man."

The next day during lunch Malik and I were walking in the hall. I decided to tell him something I had been thinking since the fair. "Dude, I'm really feeling that girl, Briana."

He nodded in agreement. "You know who she look like to me?" he asked.

I tried to cut him off. "I already know what you're gonna say…"

"Monie Love," we blurted out at the same time.

"Yeah, I had been thinking that for the longest," he noted.

85

At that point I couldn't help myself. "Bruh, she so damn cute."

"You sure you ain't 'bout to sing 'Monie in the Middle'?"

"Nah not yet, but I would." I laughed.

Malik yanked my arm. "Here's your chance, there she go with Jasmine."

"Maliiik, Deeez." Jasmine called out.

"What you screamin' for, we right here," he huffed. "That's the kind of shit I be talkin' about." Then for some reason, he walked off.

Briana chuckled. "She's loud, right?"

"Whatever, can a girl get excited?" Then she cut her eyes at him. "You know Derrick, Briana?"

"Yeah we just met. You haven't fell in anymore pools lately, have you?" She giggled.

I totally ignored her. "So, what were y'all talking about before we walked up?"

"First, we were talking 'bout your friend over there." Malik had stepped away to talk to Jay. "Girl, see how he walked off, uhhh." She stomped the ground.

"You better help him straightin' up," Jasmine warned me again. "This loving I got is too good to be taken for granted."

"Jasmine, you're funny, you need to take drama after school with me." Briana laughed.

I thought it was funny as well, but I was paying a whole lot more attention to her than to what Jasmine was saying.

The way she walked and carried herself lured me in; it was as if she didn't know how good she looked. She was going to be mine. The next time I was on the phone with Jasmine, I asked her to call Briana on three-way so we could trip out and it was on from there. Briana and I became instant friends. She was interesting and complex.

"I can tell you're not from Savannah, you talk different," I said one night on the phone.

"Yeah, I grew up in Minneapolis, everyone always says I talk white. I'm like what... I can't use proper English?"

"Nah, I ain't saying that, it's just different. I adjusted my chair and propped my feet on my dresser to relax. "Minneapolis. Isn't that where Prince is from? My brother is the biggest Prince fan ever."

"Yeah, both of my parents love some Prince – I know that *Purple Rain* album by heart."

"Brianna, you know... you're cool as hell."

"Why wouldn't I be?" she said with a slight chuckle.

"I don't know, I heard some folks say that you were stuck up."

"Yeah, I've heard that, too. I just brush it off, but sometimes it's irritating. People don't even know me like that."

"You know when folks don't see you with a boyfriend, they're gonna think you stuck up, especially since you're pretty," I said. "Just be yourself, that's why I like talking to you."

"Aww. Thanks, Dez. I'm not going to go with someone just to go with them; that's dumb. People be jumping in and out of relationships like changing clothes. I'm cool all by myself until I find someone who I think is special, you know?"

Do I? I thought.

The next day after school, I skipped out on playing basketball with the fellas to talk to her.

When I called, she picked up the phone after the first ring. "May I speak to…"

Hearing the sound of my voice she interrupted, "Hey, I was just about to walk to the store. You live close by, why don't you meet me up there?"

This was totally unexpected. The adrenaline hit and my emotions turned me into a human roller coaster.

Next, I Clark-Kented out my clothes and into something super fresh to impress her.

At this point, I knew she had to like me. I arrived at the store before her, so I paced around and thought of something nice to say when she walked up. There she was, bopping up the street, looking like my first real chance at love. She was my Tootie, my Brenda from *227*, and Charlene from *Different Strokes* all wrapped up in one girl. When she got near, my mind went blank, so I smiled and grabbed her headphones, "What are you listening to?"

"Oh, that's Neneh Cherry." She danced around, then started to sing, "No moneyman can win my love, it's sweetness that I'm thinking of…"

"Girl, what you know 'bout 'Buffalo Stance?'"

"No, what do *you* know about 'Buffalo Stance?' That's my jam." She swung her arm, pointed at me, then laughed. "I'm about to buy a Sprite and a Snickers, you coming in?"

I needed a second to collect myself. "Nah, I'll wait for you." *Big Dummy. Okay, why didn't I go in? Ask her for the go. Ask her for the go. No, take your time. Don't mess it up.* I didn't know what to do or which part of myself to listen to.

Before long, she walked out of the store, still bopping and singing as she took a bite of her Snickers.

I was glued to her moves. "What else do you like to listen too?" I asked.

She gave me a weird look. "Don't laugh but I listen to all kinds of music. I even have stuff like Bon Jovi and Metallica."

"Really, I always see the white girls in my class with those groups written on their jeans, but I never listened to it. I wouldn't mind checking it out, though. If you say it's cool." Then, I pretended to strum a guitar.

She stopped walking and turned to face me. "Dez you're really nice. You're still a bit nerdy but I think you're kind of cool."

Now I was confused. "Nerdy, huh?"

"I don't mean that in a bad way. I can tell you're smart." She pointed to her head and made a weird looking face. "You know, I should introduce you to my dad."

"Your dad?" I looked surprised.

"Yeah, I let him meet my friends all the time. I don't just introduce *anyone* to him or my mom, though. My dad has a bullshit detector out of this world." We both laughed.

The idea of meeting a parent was new to me. I'd never introduced a girl to my mom. Mostly because I didn't have a girl to introduce her to.

Should I make my move? By the time I walked her down the street I was still nervous but I did manage to grab her hand.

"Alright Dez. It was sweet of you to walk me to my neighborhood." She blushed a bit. "Guess I'll see you at lunch."

What a damn lame. I should have said something. Instead I just smiled and looked all goofy.

Still, I had walked with one of the prettiest girls at my school. Once I got in the house, I cheesed in the mirror for about five minutes. I even got my yearbook from 7th grade and pulled it out to look at her picture. *How had she gone so unnoticed? She was beautiful and tomorrow I was going to let her know how I felt.*

Then, out of nowhere, the phone rang...

Jasmine didn't even wait for me to say, "Hello."

"Dez, Dez, guess who likes you?" she asked.

I was thinking, *Okay, Brianna must have told Jasmine that she likes me. I get it, how cute*, I thought. *Ha. This was perfect. Now I could stop feeling so nervous.*

I was ready to tell her I already knew who liked me, until ...she screamed.

"Dez, my best friend, Kim likes you."

I made the ugliest face ever. "Best friend...who the heck is Kim?"

"You know her, she used to be in your homeroom. Her real name is Kalia."

Okay, hold up. Reeewind. Kalia was the girl I used to daydream about in homeroom. Mayday, we have a man down. And when I say down, I mean down like Michael Spinks after Mike Tyson knocked 'em down.

"Hello? Hello? Derrick, you there?"

And just like that, with a switch of the hips, Briana disappeared. Briana was cute, smart, different, and quite unique. However, Kalia was prime real estate. This was a woman. How could I deny myself this opportunity? I went from no girls to two girls in the matter of a day. Plus, it was only right. I had a crush on Kalia first. Shoot...

To me, the walk with Briana had confirmed our feelings. I believed she was just waiting for me to say something, but now, I couldn't stop thinking about Kalia

"So, you gon' call her?" Jasmine asked again. I think y'all would make a real cute couple."

"Yeah, I'll give her a call," I tried to say nonchalantly, but I was damn near about to jump out of my skin and die.

I looked at her number for ten minutes after I wrote it down. Then I got up from my bed and went to call her from my Mama's room. The phone was better in there and I felt that since I was handling grown folks' business, I should get comfortable on her bed and make the call.

"Hello?"

"Hello," she responded. Kalia's voice was like a goddess' to me.

"May I speak to Kalia?"

"Hi, is this Dez?" her voice massaged my ears.

"Hey, little man."

"Hey, what's up?"

After a few minutes of chit-chat she got to it. This was fine by me 'cause I didn't know what to say.

"Okay, so you know I know someone who likes you."

"Really?" I played along.

"Yeah, this person thinks you're so cute; they've been looking at you in school for a while now."

Now I was breathing hard. "Yeah, I know someone who likes you too, but they get all nervous around you."

This was all pretty crazy because we both knew we were talking about each other. However, since she liked to play it this way, I tried to learn the rules of the game quick.

"I wonder if this person really likes me."

"He definitely likes you and he has wanted you for a long, long time."

"He does?"

"Oh yes. Kalia, look, I've had a crush on you since last year, I really like you – will you be my girl?"

"Of course, I will. I liked you as well. You and your cute little walk, bopping into homeroom last year. I can't believe I'm telling you that, but it's true."

Bam, boom, zoom. I was *gone.*

The next morning, I didn't tell a soul about that conversation with Kalia. Dudes were throwing checks extra hard at the bus stop and I just let it slide. Shawn was doing his best Eddie Murphy impersonations. All he needed was a Jheri curl and a pair of tight leather pants.

"Man, y'all remember Derrick used to have that good hair? He used to come to the bus stop wit' a head full of curly hair talkin' 'bout his mama just washed it." Shawn went on, "Church, y'all hear that? Y'all hear that? But I made him confess, Lord... And he told me, 'Preacher Shawn, this ain't nothing in my hair but a Duke Kit.'"

"Why you so damn happy?" Malik asked while Shawn kept going with his joke.

I grinned and turned up the volume on my headphones. Bobby Brown was singing,

"No matter what your friends try to tell you we were made to fall in love.
And we will be together, in any kind of weather. It's like that, it's like that. Every little step..."

Yeah, I was feeling great, until I took every little step and saw Briana. Dag. During our walk, Briana and I had talked about meeting up at lunch. I knew what our unspoken word was, but when I saw Kalia, I knew she was what I wanted. I felt bad when I walked past Briana later that day holding Kalia's hand. I knew I had done something foul, but I felt she "really" couldn't hold me to anything because we never "really" said anything. I wasn't stupid though, and neither was she.

I once heard a preacher say, "We all reap what we sow." I couldn't help but feel that later on I might have regretted my choice, but not *"to-damn-day,"* I thought as I waited for Kalia by the water fountain.

She walked up to me and smiled. "Walk me to class, handsome."

Man, I had the cheesiest smile ever. It was like one of those "on a float at a parade" smiles. I was that happy and dudes around school were giving me tons of respect.

That day I heard:

"What up, Pimp?"

"Wow, you go with Kalia?"

"How you do it like that?"

"Dag, bruh, show me the game."

In my mind, I wanted to say, "Hell if I know," because I really didn't know what I had done to cause her to take interest in me. Yet, I played the role like I was the man and it felt good. So, I guessed wishes did come true.

CHAPTER 11

BONITA APPLEBUM

"Do I love you? Do I lust for you?
Am I a sinner because I do the two?
Could you let me know? Right now,
please?"

-A Tribe Called Quest

Late November 1989

The school bus arrived in our neighborhood that afternoon like a royal chariot and we stepped out as kings. The official decree was to get girls at any cost. No king wants a throne without a beautiful woman by his side.

"Hey Steve, you heard our boy Dez pulled fine ass, Kalia?" Shawn shouted for the whole street to hear. "He's been going with her for a couple days and didn't even say anything."

Steve looked preoccupied. "Man, my girl is trippin'," he mumbled.

Shawn walked in front of him and put out his hands. "Are you still going around there?"

"Nah, she said her mom might come home from work early. That means we can't do nothing." He looked pissed.

I knew sex was something teenagers probably shouldn't engage in, but now that I had a girlfriend, I had lots of questions and even more boiling desires. My dad and mom never talked about sex, so everything was left up to the world to teach me. I figured since Steve was somewhat of an expert, we should discuss details.

"What you mean, have I talked to my parents about sex?" Steve repeated like I was dumb for asking.

"Who talks to their mama about sex?" Shawn threw in his two cents.

"That's what TV's for. My dad just said be careful if you end up getting some."

"Be careful how?" I asked.

"By wearing promamatics."

"Shawn your ol' non-pronouncin' ass. The word is prophylactics, you know...rubbers...condoms," Steve barked.

"Whatever. I bet you can't spell it, even if you can pronounce it."

"That's it? I knew that...nothing else?" I asked.

"Well, what *your* daddy say?" Steve wanted to know.

Nothing, cause I didn't ask him. That's what I wanted to say, but I kept quiet instead. Maybe I should have. I mean, I did run across his stash of *Playboys* during the summer. It just felt wrong to ask.

"Hold up, you not a virgin, are you?" Steve laughed. "Cause you sound like one."

"Nah...I was just asking... cause some people think sex is bad...if you do it before you're married."

'Well, bad stuff can happen, I guess, but it damn sure don't feel bad," Shawn said with pride. "And I ain't waiting 'til I'm married."

Steve poked me in the chest. "You talk to Kalia about sex yet?"

I pushed his finger away. "I just started going with her."

"That's the perfect time." He shook his head. "For you to be so smart with some things, you sure are dumb with others."

After that, I definitely couldn't tell them I was a virgin. Although, I hoped I wouldn't be one for long.

FLICTED

Thanksgiving Break 1989

During the late 80's, a lot of hip young dudes were getting fly designs cut into their hair. I remember seeing Nike signs, stars, crazy lines and even names in graffiti letters on the back and side of heads. With that style in mind, I wanted my barber to cut a design in my hair to impress Kalia and show her how much I liked her.

I thought about it and thought about it, and the day Thanksgiving break started, I decided to do it. For this monumental endeavor, I went to Mr. Ulysses Davis' Barbershop on 45th and Bull St. I had my bright idea ready, now I had to wait for my turn to sit in the chair.

The barbershop was full of these wood carvings that were hanging up on the walls. Whenever I had to wait, I wondered how he was able to carve all the artwork that was on display. Some of the art was strange, like something out of a dream, but I did recognize the presidents and historical figures he had made.

When it was my turn, I boldly told my barber that I wanted a letter "K" cut into the back of my head.

"Are you sure? How big and what's it for?" he asked.

"It's for something special, just please make it look fresh."

When he was done, I was too proud, and I wanted everyone to see it. Well, everyone except for my mom.

Okay, now imagine this: you're young, full of yourself, living in the moment, etc., and then you walk in the house with a big-ass "K" cut in the back of your head. What do you think your mom would have done?

As I entered the house, I changed the way I normally breathed and cautiously stepped in my room to chill. I stayed in the room for most of the evening, but when I came out for dinner, my mom saw it.

"Lord, what the hell is that on the back of your head?" she asked, in shock.

My first thought was, *Ahh, mama, you don't know nothing 'bout real love and this mack I got going on* (which I definitely didn't say). Then, once I collected myself, "It's a letter 'K.'"

She looked at it from every possible angle. Then she touched it to see if it was real. "A 'K'? what does that mean?"

"It's for...this girl I go with...named Kalia," I said, yielding on every other syllable.

She took a quick look around "A girl? Go with? Go with her where?"

Before I could answer, she paused and looked like she finally understood. It was one of the first times my mom laughed at me while I was very serious. Maybe she was trying to spare my young feelings and not make me feel too dumb about it, but she was not doing a great job.

After she walked off, I immediately went to the mirror to reexamine myself.

"Man, please," I said while looking over my shoulder to see if she was behind me. As far as I was concerned, this "K" was the freshest thing I had ever done in my life. I couldn't wait to show my girl. Would she run and hug me? Would she drown me in kisses? Would she want me the way I wanted her?

Then, it hit me. *Fool, we're on break.* That meant if I didn't see her during the break, my hair would have grown back by next week. This was an official problem. I

FLICTED

had to think quick, so I called Steve to see if he had any ideas.

"Why don't y'all go to the movies on a double date with me and my girl?" he suggested.

"Bruh, you just saved my life."

"That's why you need a manager," he said, "I told you a month ago rappers can't count and keep their business straight."

"Whatever, thanks man."

****

Thanksgiving was that Thursday, and that meant a big family dinner out in West Savannah at my grandmother's. I loved seeing my family and I always had a good time eating and laughing at the craziness that took place. Before we left to go, I thought about Steve's plan and decided to call Kalia.

"Hey, I'm going to the movies on Friday, do you think you can come?"

"Uhh, I don't know, I may be doing something with my friends. Will it just be you?" She yawned. "Who else will be there?"

"You know my friend, Steve, right? We're gonna go with him and his girl."

"Cool, the only problem is my mother. She is going to trip about going way out to the Southside. Maybe I can get Jasmine to go with us. Our mothers know each other so that might make it easier for me."

Now I was beyond excited.

****

99

Thursday afternoon, we pulled up at my grandmother's for Thanksgiving. Her house was about 800 square feet, but usually when my family was packed inside, there was a lot of love. Everyone seemed ready for the festivities, but my mind was on Kalia and the movies. I got out of the car and some of my little cousins were playing in the yard while one of my older cousins was deep-frying a turkey.

Inside the house, the aroma had seeped into the walls and every piece of furniture in the dining room. Everything you touched or got close to smelt like food.

After we hugged and shouted across the room, people tried to get settled.

"Where everybody at, man, the food gon' be cold," my cousin Evette complained. She had made it in from Atlanta and was ready to eat.

"We coulda started at five in the evening for all this now," one of my uncles jumped in.

"No, what you do is tell them Negroes we gon' start at eleven, when we really gon' start at one. Then they'll be on time," my older brother Melvin added.

That made everyone laugh.

Finally, my uncle the deacon said the grace. He thanked the Lord for all we had and for pulling us through the tough times during the past year. We all held hands as he finished with, "To God Be the Glory. Amen."

Then it was on. In one trip, I grabbed some fried turkey, a heap of my aunt's famous Hudson Hill mac and cheese, and some of my other aunt's savory collard greens. I loaded up my plate with everything except for slavery food (the scraps of food they threw out to enslaved Africans that whites didn't want). Even when I was young, I could not eat chitterlings and pig feet, for nothing in the world—that shit was outta the question.

"Ahh, these brand-new niggers think they too good to eat pork, y'all," one of my older cousins shouted.

My cousin, Shareef, had tried to "drop science" over the years about pork, but it had always been a no-win situation. Hungry black people didn't care about eating healthy at Thanksgiving, even if they should.

After I ate, I sat down with Shareef and some of my older cousins to play dominoes.

"Hey Cuz, I got me a new girl." I popped the collar up on my shirt.

"Is she pretty?"

"Bruh, I'm telling you...she's the prettiest girl at my school."

"I can see how pretty she is by the way you look," he said with a grin. "Be careful, though."

"Careful...?" I stuttered.

"Yeah, don't be a sucker just 'cause she look good." After putting down his last domino, he added, "You'll be 'round here like you in love."

Hmm, what if I was... I thought, but I dared not say it.

On the way home, I couldn't stop wondering if Kalia would be able to go to the movies with me. This would officially be my first date.

When Friday came, I waited for her call all day. I checked the plug, made sure there was a dial tone, and asked my mom if she paid the bill. Then, right before it was time to go, finally, the phone rang.

"Hi Dez, look I'm so sorry, I just can't get a ride. I know you were looking forward to it. I'll make it up to you, though. I promise."

I was dead. I wanted her to see my freshly cut "sign of commitment," but I guess I wasn't that important. She made me wait all day just to tell me she wasn't coming...Thanks.

****

"Ooowee jive, Bruuuh," Steve blurted out like he couldn't believe it when he picked me up for the movies. He was the first of my friends to see the "K."

When his girlfriend saw me in line at the movies, she tried to whisper to Steve, but I could still hear her. "Okay, wow, he reeeally really like her. That "K" in his head is kinda big."

"Yeah he's gone." Steve added.

She and Steve were all over each other in the theatre and I couldn't help but think how that could have been me and Kalia.

When we got back to school that Monday after the break, my hair had grown back and you could barely see the "K."

"That's sweet but you didn't have to do that." Kalia glanced at me as I tried to show it off. "We've only been going together a few weeks."

"Yeah, I know but..."

She put her finger up to my lips to stop me from talking. "Boy, people are going to think I did something to you." Then she walked away biting her lip to keep from laughing.

This was not the outpouring of "anointed love" I was looking for. Everything with Briana had been so easy and fun. And now, for the first time, I regretted choosing

Kalia. How could she not like my cut? Was I a sucker? This is nothing like I thought it would be.

Early December 1989

It was a cold Saturday night and I had just run back home from the store like I was part of a bank heist. I turned on the tube and Ed Lover was doing this silly looking dance on *Yo! MTV Raps* when the phone rang.

"Dez, Dez, you still up?" I heard Jasmine's voice.

"Yeah, why you whispering?"

"Just in case your mama picked up."

"Okay, well, you can talk normal now." I laughed.

"Dez, guess who's spending the night at my house on Friday?"

At that moment, the world stopped. She didn't have to say who, there was only one person she would call me about. So much for regrets, huh?

I dreamed so goood about Kalia Sunday night, that I messed around and broke into a sweat. I was dead to the world. When I did wake up, I had missed the bus.

"How the heck I'ma get to school?"

I had never caught the city bus from my part of town. Now, out of necessity I had to be adventurous. Plus, there was no way I was going to call my mama at work and tell her I missed the bus. That was like asking for a free ass whooping. It was about 8:30 when I got on the CAT (Chatham Area Transit) 14B Armstrong heading into town.

"Hey, I'm trying to catch the bus to Westley Wallace Middle School, what do I do?" I asked the driver when I got on.

"Stay put 'til we make it to Henry Street; once you get there, you'll have to get a transfer."

Now from there it got confusing. I had to talk to a couple of people before I figured it out. But after a couple

104

of hours, I'd done something no one else in my neighborhood had done, and it felt good. I made it to school on my own, even though I was two hours late.

Later that day, I bumped into Jasmine on the way to class. "Are you excited about seeing your girl?"

At first I looked at her without saying a word.

Then, she got right in my face, smiled and poked me in the chest. "I know you are. Don't front."

I tried to be cool about it but, truthfully, I wanted to break out and sing like Prince Akeem from *Coming to America*. Remember when Lisa finally agreed to go out with him? "I have a date with Lisa, or, in my case, I have a date with Kalia."

"Hey, bruh, hey." Jasmine poked me to get my attention. "You straight? Your mouth was wide open. I'm talking to you and you lookin' flicted…like you blanked out."

"Nah, I'm good," I said, catching myself. "I'm going to walk around there at five."

Look, there was nothing nonchalant about it; at that point, my lil' body was on fire.

On the way to Jasmine's house, I had all this smooth Keith Sweat stuff I was going to say. Then I got nervous and didn't know what to say at all. I stopped at the store, bought a soda, and spit some rhymes to help me relax. When I walked up to the house, they were dancing in the yard. I felt like I was walking on water. Now I was finally going to do something with this girl I was crazy about.

"Hi Jasmine. Hi Kalia."

Kalia looked at me and smiled like we were in elementary school. It was coy and sweet. I had never seen her act this shy. What gives?

"Dez, you want something to drink?" Jasmine offered.

"Yeah, sure," I said, taking a glass of Kool-Aid from her hand. "Your mom don't care if you have boys around the house all the time?"

"Nah, my mom trust me; she knows I ain't doing nothing I don't pose to be doing."

Well, I want to do something I'm not supposed to be doing. "Why you and Kalia acting like y'all don't know each other?" Jasmine asked. "Y'all need some privacy?"

Kalia walked over toward me. "No, we're fine,"

I wanted Jasmine to leave, but Kalia started talking to her about any and everything. Usually around Jasmine I would be cutting up, but with Kalia I had to be cool and smooth. I wanted to let her know I was mature and could handle having a girl as fine as she was.

Eventually though, I had enough of the small talk and began to make my move, until Jasmine interrupted.

"Hey Dez, it's getting late." She handed me my coat. "My mom will be here in a few, so…"

"I thought you said she doesn't care."

"She doesn't, especially when she don't know." She smiled. "I'll let y'all say bye."

My lips were piping hot for love, but when I leaned in for a kiss, Kalia hugged me and gave me one of those grandma pecks on the cheek. I hugged her tight and my hands inched down toward her butt. *Touch it. Touch it.* Yet, before I could make a move she was waving goodbye and walking inside.

That's it? All my thoughts of passion went up in smoke.

During the long walk home, I had a serious therapy session with myself. I felt like an hour-long walk in early

December was worth waaay more than one "itty bitty" kiss. Maybe she wanted me to take the lead by doing what I really wanted and I blew it. It was no tellin' when I would see her outside of school again. Why was it so hard to be myself?

Mid December 1989

Weeks later, the temperature in Savannah began to drop and so did my love life. Something just didn't seem right between us. When we talked on the phone, it dragged and I didn't know how to make it better. Sometimes, she would yawn and make up an excuse to get off. Or, she had a bunch of homework to do. However, about a week later at the bus stop talking with Malik, my luck began to change.

"Hey Dez, you seen the previews for that movie *Glory* they filmed in Savannah?" Malik asked me.

"Nah, what's up?"

"What lil' Farrakhan talkin' bout, Dez?" Shawn butted in.

"Look Shawn, don't start that funny shit. My dad was trying to tell y'all that was Farrakhan on the Public Enemy tapes, that's all."

"Man Malik, forget Shawn, tell me what you talkin' bout?"

"My dad was talking to me about it at breakfast. It's about the Civil War and some of the black soldiers who fought in it."

"Y'all going to see it?"

"Yeah, remember Mr. Jenks and Ms. Fletcher said we were going to see it this week with our classes," he added.

"I forgot about that," I said as I turned down the volume of my headphones. "Maybe I could sit with Kalia on the bus. What you think?"

"I think they pro'lly gon' make us stay with our classes." Malik picked up his book bag as the bus approached.

"Speaking of Kalia, I always wanted to know how you ended up with her. I thought you liked Briana. When Jasmine told me y'all went together, I thought she was lying."

"Yeah, it got complicated." I shrugged my shoulders. "I'll tell you about it one day."

****

When the day came for the movies, we boarded the bus and I looked around for Kalia.

Our class got on the bus first and I saved her a seat. A lot of girls knew we went together, so when Kalia got on the bus and walked down the aisle, it felt like a mock wedding.

"Go 'head and sit with your man, girl," a group of cuties in the back of the bus shouted.

"Okay, since you all insist." She laughed, then slightly blushed.

When she sat down next to me, I knew this was my chance to take charge. I grabbed her hand and held it tightly. I felt proud and I eventually started rubbing on it which made me think I was doing something big.

Her eyes sparkled and she whispered that she liked how it felt.

In the theater, they made boys and girls sit on separate rows.

"Dag, they're so lame," I blurted out as Malik and I walked down the middle aisle. "You saw where she went?"

"Nah, I can barely see. Hold up, isn't that her coming down the aisle?" Malik motioned.

"Hey, Dez," Kalia whispered after managing to get a seat behind me. Then, she gave me a quick hug around my neck before she sat down. *If that's making it up to me, I'll take more of that.*

"Hey Kalia, your perfume smells good," I whispered back.

"You like it?"

She had no idea how much my heart was pounding. Her body had been so warm and soft. After our hug, I felt her presence linger on me for minutes.

By the time the movie started, I managed to calm down. I loved history, and seeing the power of the 54th Regiment (one of the first black group of soldiers in the Civil War) gave me a strong sense of pride. I remember the scene when Denzel Washington's character took off his shirt to get whipped. He had almost 100 lashes across his back, yet he was unafraid.

They wanted to beat him for trying to run away, when he was only looking for some shoes. The look on his face as they beat him said to me, "I don't care how many times y'all hit me. You can't break me." I felt sad when they all died in battle.

I looked over my shoulder and saw Kalia tearing up a bit, so I reached out my hand and she held it tight.

As we rode back to school, I thought what happened in the theater was a defining moment in our relationship.

I leaned in close to talk. "What did you think of the movie?"

"It was so sad, it made me cry." She sighed, still a little emotional from it.

"Yeah, it was serious. I paused and looked out the window, I really don't feel like going back to school."

Then she tapped me on the shoulder. "This feels good."

"What, the movie?" I asked.

"No, us, it actually feels like a little date." She smiled. "Are you planning to see me over the Christmas break?"

Say the right thing. Say the right thing. "Yeah, of course."

"I hope so, especially if we're going to exchange gifts." She looked to make sure I agreed.

This moment made me feel special. I figured now she was the girl for me. Now, I just needed a chance to be alone with her.

CHAPTER 12

SO WHATCHA SAYIN

"The employees of the year,
yeah we're back to work.
I took time off, while all
the rappers got jerked."

-EPMD

Late December 1989

At this point in December, the smell of Christmas trees permeated the air and lights were hanging from every house in our neighborhood. At night, you literally couldn't walk down our street without being blinded. This morning was frosty and we could see our breath taking form in the air with each word as we waited for the bus.

I rubbed my hands together before an imaginary fire, 'til I finally got fed up. "Man, I hate winter."

Malik looked at me. "This ain't nothin', Dez. I've been to Baltimore when it snows; now that's serious."

"You know what?" Steve paused. "Christmas should be in the spring, it would actually make more sense."

"Huh?" We all looked at Steve like who died and made him God.

"I'm serious," he continued. "Everybody would be out moving around celebrating instead being at home all cooped up."

"But that's not when Jesus was born," Fat said, slightly offended.

Steve huffed, "Fool, you don't know when he was born."

Since I was on a mission, I cut a hole through the laughter to talk to Malik. "Hey, never mind them, I need to hold your bike after school, that's cool?"

"You can hold it, where you going?"

"I need to ride to the mall," I said lowering my tone. "My dad sent me a little money and I want to get Kalia something for Christmas. You buying Jasmine anything?"

He sighed. "If I didn't she'd never stop talking about it.

So, after school Malik and I used their bikes and rode all the way there. I had 50 bucks to make my impression on her and I wanted to make it count. I looked in a few stores before finding the perfect silver charm bracelet that matched her style.

I pulled out the cash and Malik's eyes opened wide, "Dag, you gon' spend the whole fifty?"

"You think that's too much?"

He hesitated. "I mean I don't know, I guess…she do look good."

I was proud of what I bought and now considered myself to be somewhat of a gentleman. On the last day before the break, I strolled up to her in the hallway, and placed the gift in her hand.

"What's this?" Jasmine beamed. "Am I really that special?"

That smile, those dimples, the look in her eyes had me cheesing from ear to ear.

"I better be that important," she whispered before she melted in my arms.

A moment later she reached in her purse.

"Merry Christmas, Dez," she said handing me what had to be a wallet or a cassette tape. "Call me on the twenty-ninth, I'll be out of town until then."

I waved good-bye after another hug and made my way to the bus ramp. *Bump that,* I opened my present as soon as I sat down. She really could have placed a bow on herself and I would have been happy, but a gift was certainly cool. "Yes!" It was 3rd Bass's *The Cactus Album.* Dope.

Looking over at me cheesing, Steve noticed the tape cover on my lap. "Kalia got it for me," I said, then thought, *Damn, why did I open my big mouth.*

"Okay, how much you spent on her gift, cause tapes only cost $9.99."

"Steve man, you getting sickenin'. Why you worried 'bout all that?"

He couldn't resist taking another shot. "See, I told you rappers and money don't mix."

"If I spend money it's gotta be an even exchange and if it ain't money, it's gotta be something," he continued to counsel.

"Gotcha, Donahue. Hey, here comes our stop."

****

Three days later I was in heaven, I got this crazy fresh, Magnavox boom box for Christmas. My mom bought me a few tapes but nothing stood out like the one from my brother Rich — 2 Live Crew's *Move Something*.

The cover contained all four members relaxing in a hot tub, staring at a lady with a big-ass boonkie. Songs like "Move Something, "Do Wah Diddy" and "One & One" were all there to miseducate my young mind. And believe me, miseducate, they did.

The next day or so I was chilling in the room talking to Malik on the phone, when Rich came in.

"Hey, you know Mama 'bout to make us clean up." He shook his head. "I'm 'bout to get out of dodge. Ride to the mall with me and bring that 2 Live tape."

"Okay. What you going for?"

He popped his collar up. "It's time to get fresh again."

I told Malik I would call him back and got ready.

"Man, when I was your age, I wasn't talking to dudes on the phone, how you gon' get some talking to a bunch of boys?" He opened up the door to the car.

My face quickly filled with wrinkles. "Get some, I got me a girl."

"A girl?" he asked before pulling off. "Hold up, you not kissing on the pillows anymore?"

"Man, I wasn't ever doing that."

"Whatever, I don't believe you have a girl. Only people I hear you talking to is Malik and what's that other lil' bad joker 'round the corner, Steve?"

I rolled the window down and spit. "Man, I ain't studdin' you. I talk to girls all the time."

Once we pulled up at the mall, I got tired of being insulted and told him I was going to the arcade while he looked around.

"Alright, make sure I can find you or you will get left."

Thirty minutes had passed, and I got hungry. So, I walked to get something to eat when Kalia stepped around the corner, almost bumping into me. We were both shocked.

"Hey, I thought you were out of town," I stared at her.

"Oh hey, Dez." She looked around. "I came back early."

"You here by yourself?"

"Oh no, I'm with my big brother, I'm looking for him now."

I reached out for a hug, but she made it noticeably quick.

I was usually the nervous one, but now she was acting funny. "Did you like my gift?"

Her eyes shot down the hall. "I loved it, you have good taste. The bracelet is classy." Then she paused. "I had to hide it from my mom though...she would flip out."

"Why?"

"She thinks if somebody gives you something, then you owe them something. Isn't that silly?"

"Yeah." I halfway laughed thinking about Steve's comments on the bus.

"How long you gon' be here?"

"Just for a sec, I gotta look for my brother and he's not too cool on me having a boyfriend. So..."

"Yeah, I'm here with my brother, too, I don't think he'll be mad if he sees me with you, though." I joked in hopes she would laugh. She didn't.

Then right on cue, Rich walked up.

"Rich, this is my girlfriend, Kalia." I had never smiled so big and proud in my entire life.

"So you're actually claiming this little guy, do you know he..." I grabbed him by the arm to interrupt. "Uhhh, know he likes his girl a lot," I said nice and slow to play it off and beg him to keep quiet.

Kalia blushed, then started laughing. "Okay Dez, I'll call you later. I have to look for my brother so we can make it home." She began waving bye.

"You can't chill for a minute?"

"You don't know my brother, and I don't feel like him acting a fool."

She looked around again, then gave me another quick hug before speeding off.

When she walked away, I looked at my brother and turned up my nose. "Don't ever doubt me. What you think, she looks pretty right?"

He dapped me up. "You know, I'm not being funny, but I think I saw her a while ago with another dude."

"Nah, she's in here with her older brother."

"Oh, okay." He stiff-armed me like we were playing football. "She looks older than you, she get left back?"

I sucked my teeth and walked to the car. "Yeah, now, you're being funny."

****

When we made it home, we entered into the middle of a title bout between my mom and stepdad. My brother immediately hit an about face out the door while I entered the line of fire.

"You always hollering," she shouted as I looked out into the hallway.

"So, what you sayin', Betty?"

"What I'm saying is you don't know how to talk without yelling."

And then she yelled louder than he had yelled.

Not to be outdone, he huffed then came with it, "I'm yelling 'cause you don't like to listen and you making me repeat myself too damn much."

"Well, who are you cursing at?"

"You. And who is…" Then the conversation faded behind a closed door as they went in the bedroom for round two.

My stepdad was usually cool. He would raise his voice every now and then, but it was all bark and no bite, unless he had a little liquor to drink. He was funny, though. Sometimes he would walk around the house in his underwear with his tank top tucked into them. Whenever I saw him wear that getup, I would cough up my lungs laughing.

Even with those arguments, we still had some pretty cool conversations. Sometimes, I would catch him reading and he'd say, "You know, Dez, if I had a chance to go back in time, you wouldn't be able to pull me away from a book. Everything in life is based on what you know and if I knew then what I know now…man, oh, man."

One day, during one of his *"learn as much as you can"* speeches, he opened up an old Beach High School yearbook from the 1960s and showed me a picture of my principal from Westley Wallace. I had no idea he even knew her. He explained that they grew up together and he was amazed at all she had become.

"She was always smart and good looking, too."

He held up the book like he was checking her out. "Now, don't tell your mama I said that." Then he nudged me like I was now a member of some unofficial male-bonding club.

Anyhow, this time, he and my mom would not stop arguing once they got into the room. It got so bad that I grabbed my radio, put in EPMD, and broke out to Malik's. I left for about three hours. However, when I came back, they erupted into round three and my mom said I'd have to stay with my brother, Paul for a few days.

My big brother Paul had a big house deep in the Southside and was doing well for himself. Plus, they stayed right up the street from Jasmine.

Entering my brother's house, I sat my bags down and had just begun eating the McDonalds he bought me, when his stepdaughter, Nia came into the kitchen.

She held out her hands. "I smelt those fries from the bedroom, where mine?"

"'Sup, Niecey Pooh?" I said, grinning.

"What up, Uncle Dez? Hold up. How are you my uncle again?" she asked, and we both started laughing.

"Nothing much. Hey, let's walk and see Jasmine tomorrow."

"Definitely, I haven't been to see her in a hot minute. She still go with Malik, right?"

"Of course."

"That girl know she love that boy. She be on the bus talking 'bout her and Malik getting married and what do you think she should name their daughter."

Overhearing that, my brother put his burger down. "Long as you not talking 'bout what you're going to name yours, everything's fine."

Nia rolled her eyes so hard her pupils disappeared for a moment.

I nodded in agreement. "Yeah, she be trippin', but that's Jasmine for you..."

"Her crazy self..." Nia finished and reached for a hand full of my fries.

The next day, Nia and I walked down the street to Jasmine's house. We always had a good time being silly and when we got there, we kidded around for a while before I asked the big question. "Look, I got something I want to ask y'all."

"About?" they both asked and settled down enough to listen.

"So...when do y'all think a girl and boy are ready for taking the next step?"

"Ready for what...sex...at this age? Never!" Nia shook her head. "Uh huh, I ain't trying to get no babies..."

Jasmine looked at Nia. "Girl, you gon' wait 'til your jive get old and dusty?"

"Nah, but I do want to be married first. And all these diseases," she shivered for a moment, "Girl, no."

"Hold up, so you thinking about doing the nasty?" Jasmine asked me in shock. "Ooh, I'ma tell Kaila."

"Nah, don't say nothing." I took a big breath. "I'm just asking."

"Well, if I did do something, the boy better love me for real or I might kill him." Jasmine looked around and smirked.

Nia pushed her back on the sofa. "Girl, you ain't killin nobody."

"Huh, wait and see, I used to go with Charles Lee Ray. You remember Chucky, right?" She laughed while making repeated stab-like motions with her hand.

We tripped out 'til late that evening. Being around them made me value girls more as people. No romantic connections, just good friends. I kind of wanted to feel how I felt with them with Kalia. Free to talk and not worry about being perfect.

The next day, my brother took me back to the war zone. He said my mom and stepdad had called a truce and for now, all was well.

"How was it at Paul's?" my mom asked when I walked in.

I yawned, still sleepy after staying up late talking with Nia. "Everything was cool… hey mama, you mind if I walk to Shawn's?"

"That's fine, but 'fore you leave, I need you to go through some mail for me and read a few things."

"Read?" *Ahhh, man, how lazy can you be.* I honestly felt she was taking advantage of her free child slave labor and I was blowed. Between fetching the remote control, getting drinks out the fridge, and running to the store, I had an attitude about being a miniature butler.

I'm ready to go, I said to myself, while she talked. Being at home felt like being in a cage.

She wanted me to read something for her and I should have just done it, but I had no idea the depth of her request. Then in the middle of my duties, the phone rang.

"Hello, it's for you," my mom said, holding out the phone to me. "Some lil' girl. Hurry up."

"Hey, what's up?"

"Dez, you okay?" Kalia asked. "You sound weird."

Once I got to my room and closed the door, I continued talking. "Nah stuff just been crazy 'round my house with my mom and stepdad."

"I hope things will be okay. I'm sorry about the other day at the mall. I was calling to tell you I'm going to perform in the MLK Day parade. I wanted you to come and watch me. Maybe we can spend some time together." She paused. "Oh, and I have another present for you."

Another present, what could it be? I knew what I was hoping it was.

This was just what I needed.

CHAPTER 13

YOU MUST LEARN

> *"Teach the students what*
> *needs to be taught. Cause black*
> *and white kids both take shorts.*
> *When one doesn't know about the*
> *other one's culture, Ignorance*
> *swoops down like a vulture."*

-Boogie Down Productions

Mid-January 1990

The sun woke up and poured bright yellow rays all over the city. I didn't want to get up, but my alarm clock kept going off. Then I heard my mom and stepdad fuss while she cooked breakfast.

"How you spent that much money without asking me?" my stepdad yelled.

"Ask? Hold up. That's not even your money. The money Dez gets has nothing to do with you."

"How it don't?" my stepdad demanded to know. "It's all ours."

123

"No, so you can mismanage it and take it." She was so angry she knocked the carton of eggs on the floor, cracking most of them.

"Take it, huh? You're welcome to pay all the bills."

"I could do a better job than you," she said and turned up her nose.

As I walked out the house for school, I couldn't help but wonder...*Is this what love is?* I never argued with Kalia, so maybe that was a good sign, right? I knew I didn't want to grow up and be like them.

That day, from the moment we got off the bus 'til the bell rang for first period, my friends and I argued about football.

Malik didn't hesitate to get under my skin. "Hey, what you think 'bout them Steelers, Dez?"

"He don't think nothin' after them boys lost to Denver," Mr. Two Cents, Shawn added.

"Outta there. Go home. See ya," Malik continued.

"Man, your team ain't even in it. Least we had a chance," I snapped.

When we were in the hall, Mr. Jenks heard us heavily debating who would win it all.

"Are you sure you don't own or play for the team?" he asked with a grin. "No? Okay, well, since you don't, can we move on to something just a little more important?"

"He just mad cause he can't catch," I told Shawn.

"He can catch that food though, look at his stomach," he said, pointing at Mr. Jenks's mid-section.

Mr. Jenks knew we were being silly, so he ignored us. Then he cleared his throat and read a Dr. King quote to start class: *"The function of education is to teach one to think intensively and critically. Intelligence plus character— is the goal of a true education."*

"We all know how to think, Mr. Jenks." Brian, who was still recovering from the last time he and Mr. Jenks got into it, laughed.

"But do you know how to think critically?" Mr. Jenks replied. "For example, do you think people are really thankful for what King and so many others did? Or do you think we take them for granted?"

"Take them for granted?" A girl in my class said while screwing up her face, "I don't know them." A lot of people laughed.

"Nah, he means what they did for our whole society. I understand what he's trying to say," Shawn jumped in.

"I guess we should keep fighting for the things they stood for," my friend, Mya pondered.

"I got you, Mr. J," I started. "You're trying to tell us that we could at least go to the parade or see what some of the new issues are, right?"

"Bam, there you go. Some of you are ready to think critically."

"Mr. Jenks, you heard about Robbie Robinson getting murdered?" I asked. I talked about it with my stepdad the month before.

Everybody started to chime in all at once, though a few people in my class looked clueless.

"Yes, I do, it's really sad." Mr. Jenks nodded. "For those of you who don't know, he's the NAACP lawyer who was killed by a mail bomb this past December. He was also one of the first black students to help desegregate Savannah High School."

"They can send a bomb in the mail?" Shawn asked.

I was mad enough about the murder to explode. "Yes, my stepdad said the bomb blew off his arms, and then he died in the hospital a few days later."

Mr. Jenks paused and looked down for a moment. "He stayed right up in the street from our school in Liberty City and he left behind a wife and kids,"

Many people wondered out loud, "Why would someone do that?"

"According to the news, a white supremacist named Walter Moody sent it to him."

Brian looked at Mr. Jenks. "Now that's something I would definitely want to march about."

"Me too, man." I dapped Brian up in support.

Later during class, I finished up my work and started skimming through a book Mr. Jenks had on display in the room. In the book, I saw a picture of downtown Savannah and decided to read the rest of the page. It stated that in 1964, Dr. King said, "Savannah was the most desegregated city in the south," and since I was from Savannah I wanted to know why. My stepdad read a lot and grew up during that time, so I figured I would ask him when I got home. On the bus, I threw on my headphones and zoned out.

"I got a tool known as a forty-four with an impact that could break down a door. Now, why don't you think I can't break down the law, if the laws corrupt as the President I saw..."

I was kickin' YZ's new song, "Thinking of a Master Plan."

Raps like these inspired me to write and helped me to look at the world differently. I came in from school, threw my books on my bed and went in search of my stepdad. I found him in the kitchen eating a sandwich.

"Hey Phil, you ever heard Dr. King say anything about Savannah?" I asked him.

"About Savannah? No, I'm not sure... did he?"

I told him what I saw in the book.

"I never knew that," my stepdad said, "It does makes sense," he nodded. "Before I went in the Navy, I remember how Black people in Savannah had protested and held boycotts of white stores. We shut down Morrison's, Levy Jewelers, and many others on Broughton Street. That forced the city government to change things in '61 before it got wild like what went down in Birmingham and other Southern cities."

"Sounds like folks were real organized."

"We must have shut down at least fifty white-owned stores and everyone was even talking about not buying anything during Christmas. See, when you start messing with the money, white folks are willing to change things quick," he finished.

"Wow, if people wouldn't have bought anything around Christmas, stores would have definitely felt that."

"Exactly. So, you do have a brain when you not doing all that rap stuff." He laughed.

"Did Dr. King ever come to Savannah?"

"I'm not sure, but there were plenty of strong leaders here. Remember as great as MLK was, he didn't do it alone. In Savannah, there was this man named Hosea Williams, who was fiery and militant. W.W. Law, who your school was named after and there was a young dude we all knew named Benjamin...I think his last name was

Clark. Yeah, Van Clark, and they called him the little general. He was around seventeen."

"Seventeen? That's young," I said, almost in disbelief.

"Young people had direction back then. I'm not saying we were perfect 'cause we weren't, but a lot of us wanted to get involved and just make something of ourselves," he added.

"Wow, I had no idea. Thanks for dropping that knowledge on me."

"Dropping knowledge?"

"Yeah, teaching me," I yelled as I ran out the door to hang out with my friends.

****

That weekend, I decided to go to the parade partly because I didn't want to take things for granted, but my main reason was obviously Kalia. I had to see her. She was performing and I wanted my present. I just had to figure out how to get there.

On Monday morning, the day of the parade, I got up early. I cleaned up and got out of the house quickly. Next, I stopped by Steve's. He and Shawn were outside playing basketball.

I knocked the ball out of Shawn's hands. "Y'all trying to go to the parade?"

Shawn chased the ball down then threw it at me. "Yeah, how we gon' get there? We need a ride."

"We don't need a ride, we can catch the CAT," I said, now that I was an expert. "Look, all we gotta do is catch it downtown. We can walk from Abercorn over to MLK like it's nothing."

"Bet, I'm with it," Steve said.

"Cool, I'm in, too," Shawn said.

So, with that, Steve, Shawn, and I trooped downtown to the parade.

"Hey, I ain't trying to be disrespectful, but damn your girl fine. I know it be other dudes trying to talk to her," Steve said as we passed by the mall.

"Nah, Steve, you ain't being disrespectful, that's exactly what I want to hear from my boy," I said in an exaggerated tone.

Steve pointed to a light skin girl on the bus. "Boy, if Kalia was red like her, she would have dudes lined up around the block."

"If she was red? She looks fine the way she is."

"How you don't like dark skinned girls," Shawn sucked his teeth, "but you're dark skinned."

Steve looked up in the sky like we were dumb. "Y'all ain't never heard of opposites attract?"

I had enough at that point. "Man, all girls are beautiful. I don't trip off skin color."

"Okay, bump all that, you done got some or what?" Steve stood up to press me for an answer.

I used my arm to push him away. "I'm doing what I do, and this is our stop. Let's get off."

He couldn't stop laughing. "Shawn, that means no."

"Okay, to be honest, I barely had a chance to be alone with her."

"C'mon, you ain't gotta chance to feel on her boonkie or nothing?"

'Look, I'm working on it," I said as we crossed Montgomery Street en route to the parade.

Shawn started breathing hard. "Hey man, slow up, I know you want to see your girl, but dag you 'bout to make me break an ankle."

"I'm surprised you haven't said anything about the dance coming up next month."

"Dance?"

"I thought you knew – everybody been talking about it. All the honeys will be fresh dressed and lookin' fly. Just think of all the girls we gon' be able to dance with. And when them lights get low for them slow jams, boy."

By this point, we were in the heart of the parade. Everybody in the crowd was smiling. The food was piping hot and bands were in full swing. I loved to see the high school marching bands dance while they played. A drum major stepped to the front and blew on his whistle. They were ready to throw down.

"Savannah High always has the best marching band," Shawn shouted over the drums.

"Hey, y'all heard 'bout the Givens Gang?" Steve asked.

I was clueless. "Who that, some kind of rap group?"

"Nah, one of my cousins was telling me about them. Them boys be poppin' folks."

Shawn cut in, "Yo, there go your girl, Dez."

"Where?" My head spun around.

"Right there, marching…"

Yep, she was all mine, and every time she shifted her hips, my heart floated.

She waved to me from the middle of the street in the parade and I felt like a king. My friends were so jealous. Both of them were gawking at my girl.

After she passed by, we walked around for a while before I headed to the end of the route to try and see her.

"Dag, you seen where they went?" I asked looking in every direction except for behind me.

"Huh hum," Shawn coughed to get my attention.

Kalia walked up behind me and covered my eyes with her hands. "Hey y'all."

"Ms. Sims." I smiled, once I heard her voice.

"Look, I wish I had more time," she said, rushing over her words," I just wanted to give you a quick hug. My coach is gon' flip out if I don't stay with our group."

She pulled me close and I smelled that perfume again and that hug made me damn near melt.

"I'll call you later," she whispered. "Bye y'all."

"Uh oh, Dez, that looked serious." Steve continued to gawk. "Imagine if she lived close enough for you to walk to her house."

"Nah, I can't imagine that 'cause I would lose it…hell, I'm losing it now."

"See, little Dez." Steve paused to clear his throat. "When you have a girl that lives close by, you can go see them almost anytime," he bragged. "Anytime my girl mama goes to work… I'm there."

"Yeah, I hear you," I said, but I was still stuck on her outfit and those sequins that went up and down her body. This was torture to see her and be limited to hugs.

All in all, I was glad we went. A little after noon, the parade winded down and we made our way back home. Walking past Bull Street, we headed towards Abercorn to catch the bus, when a speeding patrol car hopped up on the curb next to us.

"Stop! Stop! Freeze!" the officers shouted, jumping out of the patrol car.

"Freeze? What did we do?" I asked, almost too shocked to move.

"I said freeze." And then one of the officers pulled out his gun.

"Someone said they saw some young guys trying to break into some cars over on Jefferson Street. You all know anything about that?" His gun maintained aim.

"Well that wasn't us," Steve barked, in a tone that also said, *"Man look at this bullshit."* He added, "We're coming from the parade."

"Y'all have any ID?" the officer said, as he tried to read our body language for clues.

Steve was about to lose it. "ID? Man, we're fourteen..."

"Without proof, we don't know jack. I need everyone's names, and I want you to put your hands up against the car."

Though we were innocent, I was nervous. I started to fidget and twitch. Shawn whispered for me to stay cool. I didn't want to go to jail and I'd gone to the parade without telling my mom. I could hear her voice now.

The scene was beginning to turn for the worse. Steve and one of the officers started to argue about him keeping his hands on the car, when I heard a familiar voice.

"Excuse me, officers, I know these young men. They're no criminals, what happened?"

After a couple of moments of explaining, showing them his ID, and them calling headquarters, the police left.

"Mr. Jenks, boy, I'm glad to see you," I said, breathing a sigh of relief.

Shawn's normal comedic tone was gone. "When I lived in Yamacraw, I used to see stuff like this happen all the time. People got accused of stuff and harassed by cops like it was nothing. I guess it doesn't matter where you live when you're black."

Mr. Jenks shook his head like he knew something foul could have happened. "Yeah, those officers looked like they wanted y'all to be guilty."

Steve was still hot. "Cops be trippin', man. That's why I don't like em. What if Mr. Jenks hadn't come?" Steve asked, with his blood boiling over.

I agreed. "Yeah, ain't no tellin'. I know all cops ain't bad, but we could have been killed."

"I wrote down his name and badge number," Mr. Jenks said. "I have some friends who work at the precinct that I am going to report it to."

This let me know just how expendable we were. We could have died without a moment's notice and no one would have been able to do anything. Mr. Jenks saw that we were shook up and searched for the right thing to say. "I'm sorry that happened to y'all." He grabbed Shawn and I by the shoulders. "Always do what they say until it's over." He paused like he hated to say what he was saying but knew that he had to. "Then once you get out of the situation, you can figure out your next move. Steve, I love your will to fight, but you can't fight if you are dead." Then he paused and looked at us again. "Y'all were coming from the parade, right?"

Steve sucked his teeth and spoke up. "Yeah, we were on our way to catch the bus."

"Well, hop in, y'all can ride back home with me."

After we drove through a few stoplights, we tried to blow the incident off by changing the subject. Otherwise, no one would have said another word.

Steve patted Mr. Jenks on the shoulder. "No, what are you doing for Valentine's... I know you trying to get some loving."

"What do you know 'bout some loving?" he asked as he adjusted the rear-view mirror to look at Steve. "Yes, I'm definitely going to do something special for my...WIFE."

I smirked at his response. "Say, Mr. Jenks, you ever argue with your old lady?"

"Of course, he do. Everybody does, bruh. That's just a part of it," Shawn jumped in.

"Well, it is a part of it, but if you love someone, you learn to make it work without arguing all the time," Mr. Jenks added.

"In other words, Dez, his wife be in there slappin' that head up," Shawn said.

Even Mr. Jenks had to laugh at that.

"Now, you know better than that, boy. My wife and I have an understanding and we just make sure we put God first. That's not always easy, but it keeps us doing the right thing even when we may not want to."

"You just got married?" Steve asked Mr. Jenks.

"Yes, but hold up. Did I miss something? Why are y'all so concerned with marriage all of a sudden?"

Then Shawn had to say it, "Man, that's Dez thinking 'bout Kalia."

"Who, Kalia *Sims*?" Mr. Jenks said, like he was in shock. "Derrick, you go with Kalia?"

"Yeah, I been going with her for a little over two months."

"Ahh no, not little Dez," he said, clowning me with this Santa Claus-sounding voice. "You got you a lil' girlfriend, huh? Now, you know I'm going to mess with

134

her when I see her. She could do so much better than you," he joked as we pulled up to my house.

"Whatever. Matter fact, let me out now. I'll see y'all tomorrow."

I spent the rest of the night dreaming about the school dance. Me and Kalia, holding each other. Close. Real close.

"Don't be afraid of the way you feel. Open your heart and you'll see it's real.

We whispered along with Skyy as they sang the new jam "Real Love."

CHAPTER 14

TEENAGE LOVE

*"Hey, sport, here's a
thought from the old-school
crew. A serious situation we
all go through.*

-Slick Rick

February 1990

After two months of trying to figure out this thing called love, the one and only Kalia was still mine. Seeing her at the parade felt like a part of my destiny. So why the heck did I miss Jasmine? With her, I never had to think twice about what I wanted to say. I was accepted with every inch of my natural goofy self and I loved it. I remember one time we called a dude in her class with this really bad prank idea.

"Dez, I bet you won't act like you're his girlfriend," Jasmine dared me.

Always ready for a dare, I quickly made my voice change to one with a real high pitch.

"Hey, is this Kendrick's mama? Okay, I just wanna let you know Kendrick got me pregnant, and my mama wanna know what he gon' do."

As I was saying this foolishness, I heard Jasmine cracking the paint on her walls from laughing. Still, I wouldn't break character for nothing.

"Whaaaat. He got you pregnant? No lord, no." And the phone went silent.

"Hello, hello…"

"Dez, I think she fainted. Did you hear how she sounded?"

I laughed. "Dag Jasmine, I feel kind of bad…"

"I don't…if she believe that jive, then she's dumb."

We were nuts.

Anyway, I was now focused on Valentine's Day. It was approaching fast and everyone was talking about their dates and what they were planning to wear to the dance.

I had barely turned the corner from Mr. Jenks's class when Jay and Shawn ran up to me laughing.

Shawn slapped the wall and howled. "Boy, Malik and Jasmine just got into it."

"Dude, it was crazy," Jay said. "I thought he was about to slap her. I don't know what she did, but she did something 'cause he was steaming mad."

Shawn leaned on the wall. "Jay, did you see how she was waving her hands in his face?"

"Yeah, I gotta talk to him, I can tell he was embarrassed." Jay looked down the hall for him. "If you have to argue and carry on with someone like that, it's not worth it."

After that, everyone in the 8th grade knew they were pretty much done. *What could have caused it?* Finally, on the way home from school that afternoon, he decided to say something.

"Hey, I know you heard," Malik started.

"Yeah, what's up with you and Jasmine?" I asked real easy.

"Man, she just getting sickening. That girl acts like talking on the phone with somebody all night mean that you love them...not to mention, all that up on me jive at school. Man, I need a little space," he barked. "She got mad because I didn't call her back yesterday. I told her I didn't feel like talking and she started yelling and carrying on about some other girl who's supposed to like me. I don't even know this other chick."

****

A couple of days later, Jasmine called and said they broke up, but she wanted to go back with him. Then they broke up three or four more times during the month before they did it for good. Meanwhile, Kalia and I were beginning to really connect.

"Hey Dez, guess what?" She walked up to me at lunch. "Yesterday, I was with my mom buying a hot dress for the dance. Aren't you excited?" She twirled around like the dress was in her hands.

"Yeah, I was talking to Shawn about it the other day. You're going to be the finest girl there." I moved her bang back from out of her eye. She smiled and winked at me.

Later that night on the phone, we continued to talk about the dance and our upcoming eighth grade trip. Every year our school went somewhere, and this year we were headed to Orlando. I imagined Kalia at the beach and thought about what we could do until my mom and stepdad cranked up an argument. *Do they ever stop?* It seemed like the usual stuff at first, but then, suddenly, my mom screamed. "Don't grab my damn arm. I done told you it bothers me. People make me crazy when they grab me—let go," she demanded.

Well, he didn't let go and the next thing I knew, there was a loud boom. I looked in the hallway from my room and my mom was laid out flat on the floor. *Hold up. I know this dude ain't hit my mama.* Then, before I could figure out what to hit him with, my stepdad yelled out, "Dez, watch your Mama. I'm calling the ambulance; she done passed out."

"Kalia, I gotta call you back."

"What's up, that was loud...you okay?"

"I gotta call you back," I stuttered before finally getting it out.

I quickly went to inspect my mother. I stood over her and her eyes popped open like a cuckoo bird coming out at noon. She stared at me, then closed and reopened her eyes several times as if she was speaking in code.

After he called 911, my stepdad called my brother, Melvin. Melvin pulled up right after the ambulance did, and he came in noticeably upset. With a slight grimace, Melvin looked down at my mama to be sure she was all right and then she opened her eyes again.

"Hey, ain't nothing wrong with me, fool. I gotta teach him a lesson since he won't stop drinking and yelling," she whispered.

I looked at Melvin and he looked at me, we were blowed. I shook my head as the paramedics checked her out. Then, I called Kalia back and told her what happened.

"Was she alright?" she asked, sounding alarmed.

"Did you not hear what I just said?"

"Okay, y'all are crazy." She laughed. It was time for her to get off the phone, so she blew me a little kiss and said goodnight.

The very next day at lunch, I was looking for Kalia everywhere. I even skipped eating just to spend extra time with her. Yet, she was nowhere to be found. While I looked around clueless, a friend of mine from class named Ron walked up.

"Hey, Dez, you know I go up to Windsor after school?" he started. "I'm a ball boy for the basketball team."

"Oh, yeah, I remember Malik mentioned it to me. That's cool, you trying to get in good with the coach, huh? And you get to see Daryle Wall play. I heard he's the best player in the city since Pervious Ellison."

"Yeah, he is. I've seen him hit crazy shots at practice." With that, he took a breath, then held his head down a bit. "Dez, you ever heard of a dude named Chop?"

"Who? Man, what kind of name is Chop?" I asked.

"Shoot, I don't know, but his real name is Byron," he said. "Anyway, he's always asking me about his girlfriend."

"Look, Ron, what does that have to do with me, bruh?" I said losing patience as I peeked over his shoulder to look for Kalia.

"Well..." he said real slow, "your girl is his girl."

"Huh?"

FLICTED

He put his hands on my shoulder and looked at me. "Yeah bruh, listen, he goes with Kalia."

My chest suddenly cramped up. "Are you sure? Nah, it's got to be another girl. Not her."

Ron continued to put the knife into my heart. "Yes, I'm sure. He asks about her every day and she gave me a note for him."

The look on my face was like I got hit by a Mac truck. I was crushed. I couldn't believe it. I actually waited a whole week before I said something. I was so happy she was my girlfriend that I guess I wanted to enjoy her for a little longer; which was pretty pathetic. Finally, I couldn't take it. So, I wrote her a letter.

Dear Kalia,

You can't possibly know how I feel. Imagine my surprise when Ron told me my girl has another boyfriend. I've known for a while, I just wanted to see how much you would lie to me. You broke my heart in 100 pieces. Why? What did I do? It's okay though, I'm the big dummy. Thanks.

I had to stop there. I mean, it wasn't like I could tell her how I really felt. Imagine me saying,

Hey, you know what, you're actually my first girlfriend, my first. You meant a lot to me. I loved you. Shit, do you know I gave up going with Briana to go with you?

"Old biscuit head-ass girl," I yelled out in my room. I was mad, sad, and tired of looking like I had actually done something wrong. Even though the relationship had its challenges, she was special to me. I was so into her, I hadn't even been practicing my flows. For her, I was probably just a little dude with no game whom she decided to give a chance for, who knows what reasons.

She wrote a note back.

Hey Derrick,

Look, I am very sorry for hurting you. I admit everything is true and I'm sorry you had to find out that way. You're too nice of a guy for me to keep lying to. Anyway, it was nice while it lasted. Take care. You can still be my friend if you want.

*If I want...*I asked myself as my brain swelled with rage. *This chick has a lot of nerve.* All my big plans were gone, like that.

****

When the day of the dance came, we were all ready, but we got dressed up and didn't even have a ride. That evening, we sat outside Steve's, thinking of a way to get there.

"What about Malik or Fat?" I asked Steve.

"Nah, none of them are going."

"Fat staying home to talk to his make-believe girlfriend and I thought you saw Malik." Shawn laughed.

"He hurt his leg in gym class." Desperate, Shawn paused.

"Somebody told me Will's going. Maybe we can all ride with him."

I didn't hesitate for one second. "Let's go." There was no way I was missing this party.

After five minutes of non-stop running, we slowed down as we made it to the entrance of his neighborhood.

"Damn, I'm tired." I attempted to catch my breath.

Steve was already upset. "These hoes better look good, we up here running and shit."

"Why they gotta be hoes, though?" I laughed.

"You know what I mean...girls, tricks, damsels in distress... it's all the same."

"Hey Steve," I looked at Shawn like he was slow, "tell this man Humpty Hump and Shock G from Digital Underground are not the same person."

Shawn shook his head. "I'm telling you I saw the video and my cousin who lives in LA said they're twins."

"Put some money on it." Steve smirked.

Will's dad's car was still in the driveway, which suggested he hadn't left yet, so we knocked on the door.

"'Sup, fellas?" Will held out his hands. "Y'all need a ride, I can tell. Why didn't y'all just call? I could have asked my dad to pick you up."

"Shoot, I don't know...Dez was like let's go and we all ran..." Shawn looked back at me like it was pretty dumb.

"Hell, you followed me, you could have said stop."

"Who y'all planning on dancing with?" Will asked as he opened the car for us to get in.

Steve started running his mouth, while Shawn whispered, "I heard you and Kalia broke up."

Well, damn, my business travels fast, but I don't know how, I didn't tell any of my friends.

143

Will interrupted. "My bad, y'all, the back doors don't open." He looked embarrassed about his dad's car. "I'm gonna have to climb over the front seat."

Will's dad had a big spaceship-lookin' Lincoln Continental. Once he opened the door, I clapped my hands twice. "Yes, Chauffeur, to the Windsor?"

We were all acting highfalutin, only to sit down and see that *there was no back seat.* Now, under normal conditions, we would have checked the shit out of him about this crazy contraption of a car. However, we needed a ride. "My nigga, where the seats at?" Steve said, with no regard for Will's dad.

"Man, who cares?" Shawn said, looking out the window to laugh.

We wanted to go so badly that we squatted on the floor of the car and made our way there. We were in that Lincoln piled on top of each other, comforted by visions of becoming men.

When we drove up to venue for the dance, Bobby Brown's "My Prerogative" was blaring and all the girls looked too good in their Valentine outfits. Briana, Mya, and all their friends looked real fly. I couldn't wait to do this Kid 'n Play kick step routine I had practiced with Steve. You couldn't tell us we weren't the liveliest dudes at the party. Suddenly, the DJ threw on Digital Undergrounds jam, "Humpty Dance."

"Now stop what you're doing
'cause I'm about to ruin
the image and the style that you're used to."

144

That place went buck wild with a room full of teens all doing the same dance move. I couldn't believe how much fun we were having. Then *bam!* I saw Kalia. She looked gorgeous and was so much of a little woman, I couldn't help but fall for her all over again. I hadn't spoken to her since the break-up, a week ago, and my feelings were all over the place.

I was still mad, but I wanted to speak. Maybe it would be nice to dance with her after we spent three whole months being an item.

Yet, every time I started walking toward her my pride gave me a reason not to. To make it worse, that night, she danced with Shawn (*what a sellout*) and a white dude I used to be good friends with in elementary school.

Everyone at the party looked at me. They knew I had been dissed hard.

I acted like I didn't care but I did. We had just hit the neighborhood on the way back when I started to feel it. I had lost my girlfriend who had looked so, so, *so good* that night and a single tear rolled out of my right eye. I had thought if I ignored her, that somehow, she would beg me to take her back. Man, that heifer didn't even look my way.

As I sniffled a couple times, I saw Steve slowly turning to look at me. "Hey, y'all, this nigga back here crying."

I tried hard to wipe the tears away, but they ran around my face, avoiding my hand at all cost. It was as if my tears said, "Nah, bruh, we're about to make sure everybody sees this."

Everybody in the car looked at me and I was willing to bet none of them had ever seen a dude cry over a girl.

"See, that's why I don't follow them skeezers up; Shawn, you see this?" Steve said.

I got out the car and Shawn tried to dap me up, but I walked off without a word. I got home, put on some slow songs and just stared at the ceiling. It felt like the longest night of my life when I broke down and cried some more. Snot bubbles and tears gushed out everywhere.

The next morning at the bus stop, I knew it would be hard to escape the jokes.

"Bruh, say it ain't so. Them boys talkin' 'bout you cried after the dance. For real?" Malik asked.

"I told him, we 'posed to make hoes cry, not be a hoe," Steve said.

I was fuming.

"Well, look at it this way, bruh: it could be worse. At least you found out now instead of later. You could say it was a blessing in disguise," Malik joked.

I stood there with a blank stare, "Real funny..." For better or worse, I had tasted how great and how bad so-called love could be. Now I had to find some way to live it down.

CHAPTER 15

IF IT ISN'T LOVE

"I don't love her.
I tried to tell myself.
But you can see it in my eyes.
So don't deny
I can't fool no one else.
The truth is in the tears I cry. "

-New Edition

Late Feb 1990

"Boy, who said you can sing, and why are you singing anyway?" my mom questioned as she looked into my room. "It's Saturday and you in here up under the covers, what's going on?" She snatched the blankets off my bed like the finale of a magic trick. "You've been doing this the whole week."

I wanted to tell her about my ordeal and that love had reduced her son to this pitiful state, but I didn't know where to start. I was moping around the house playing "If It Isn't Love" and some stupid Wilson Phillips song that kept coming on Z-103. I'm using the word singing loosely because it really was more like crying.

If that wasn't bad enough, Monday morning I started feeling nauseous. I really wanted to stay home, but my mom gave me an Alka-Seltzer Plus Cold tablet and told me to carry my behind to school. This was pretty much her remedy for everything.

"Mama, my throat hurts."

"Take a Cold Plus."

"Mama, I fell off my bike and broke my arm."

"Boy, you better take a Cold Plus."

The night before, I had gotten into a big argument with my brother, Rich. My mom didn't feel like taking me to the barbershop and she asked—or rather, *made*—him cut my hair.

"Bruh, what you doing?" I asked, since he was cutting my hair real aggressive.

"Man, lil' joker, hold still," he warned.

When I looked at my tapeline in the mirror, I almost passed out. "Man shit. You did that jive on purpose, *damn.*"

"I bet you won't ask me no mo'. Remember my jeans?"

He made a good point; however, I was in no mood to negotiate. I tried to box him in the face, but he caught my arm and held me down while I huffed and puffed awhile. The edges of my hair looked like a crumbled cookie—no straight lines whatsoever. Still, I had to go to school.

Now I was the sucker who cried with a jacked-up haircut.

When I arrived at the bus stop that next Monday morning, I felt like God was playing a joke on me and maybe I would wake up soon.

FLICTED

Fat was the first to notice. "Dag, your hairline is jacked up. Who cut that shit like that?"

I explained what happened and he expressed his condolences. "Yeah, you should have told that fool never mind. Your head is dead."

Then he turned around and yelled, "Hey y'all. Look a' Dez tapeline."

Even some of my white friends at the bus stop were laughing.

"Oh, it's like that?" I said, looking at Fat like he was Judas.

"Bruh, I owe you. You stay with something slick to say. Don't get mad now," he hollered out.

"I ain't mad, Fatman, I know you got a good luck sandwich in one of your socks, though."

"A sandwich? Aw, man, that was corny. You coulda saved that." He pointed to my tapeline again.

I wanted to get back at him but didn't have the energy, so I let him have it. Since my image was tarnished, I walked around that day with my head under my sneaker soles. By the time I stepped in Mrs. Fletcher's door, I didn't want to be bothered at all. Ol' Fletcher was my third period teacher. She had a real chipper white southern belle charm about her and she taught this new class called Leadership.

"Why are we in this class again?" I asked my home girl, Angela.

She sat up straight in her desk. "I guess we're supposed to be smart."

"Well I haven't been feeling so damn smart lately."

"Yeah, I heard what happened with Kalia, player, it happens to the best of us."

"Thanks, I think…" I wondered if she heard we broke up or that I cried, but I wasn't going to ask to find out.

"What are we supposed to be doing today? You know?"

"Uhh, that big project we have been working on for weeks." She paused and giggled. "Well, I've been working, I don't know what you've been doing."

"Nothing, I don't take this class seriously, they just made this jive up. They should give us a grade for coming." I took out my rap notebook. "Hey Angela, can I see your headphones?"

"See, yes. Hold them, no. You almost got my stuff taken last time."

"You talking about me, what are you doing?" I looked at the notebook on her desk. "You ain't working on no project."

"Nah, I'm writing, you know I be flowing." She acted as if she had a mic in her hand.

"Man, I thought I had a lot of rhymes, you got me beat." I pulled my desk toward her. "I haven't heard you rap since the beginning of school. Let me hear something?" I asked.

"I can't rap in class, but you can read it, I guess."

The girl Lo-lo,
I'm the symbol of quality.
Stop me,
you must be outcha psychology???
rappers press up, now owe an apology
for wasting my time, I mean honestly.

I couldn't believe a girl had that much skill. I liked Salt-N-Pepa growing up and MC Lyte was fresh beyond words, but Lo-lo was the first female I knew personally who had real talent.

I was in the middle of reading another one of Lo-lo's raps when Mrs. Fletcher came over. "You are going to do some work in my class today, Mister 'I'm too cool for school.'"

"I'm doing my work, Mrs. Fletcher."

"Well, where is it?" she demanded.

"Here, there, I don't know, musty girl, everywhere."

Her mouth was wide open but nothing came out. She was shocked. "Why do you think you can disrespect me?" She stomped her foot and the heel of her shoe flew off.

"It's really disgusting and childish how you act. One day you'll look back and regret it, and that's a promise."

After that, she drew an imaginary exclamation mark in the air with lightning speed and dotted it like her finger was on fire. Me, I kept on laughing as if she was a joke.

"I'ma do the work, lard boonkie, chill out."

"Lard...did you just call me lard?" she said as her face turned bright red.

"Well actually I said lard boonkie."

"That's gonna earn you a day at home."

Mrs. Fletcher was furious and after we exchanged some more words, she sent me to Mr. Jenks. I wish I could have said the situation at home or my breakup had influenced me, but in truth, I had just started to change. I mean, I was always a bit of a jackass when I wanted to be, but now my social life officially mattered more than my education.

"She acts like this man my daddy," I huffed on the way to see him. He was also the youth minister at my church and we had grown very close.

"What's going on with you?" he asked sternly. "You been acting funny lately. I hope it's not because of that girl."

"Huh?"

"Yeah, I heard like everybody else." He threw up his hands. "Shawn told me."

"Nah man, it ain't 'bout no girl, I just don't like Ms. Fletcher, and she doesn't like me."

"Well, let's see. Do you do what she asks you? Like, your work?"

"No," I begrudgingly admitted.

"Well, that might be a big cause of your problems." He tapped the wall with his fist. "Look, don't make her keep coming to get me. You're making yourself look like a little boy, plus it's sickening. Just do your work. Besides, we both know your mama will kill you."

And he wasn't lying. The last time I had gotten a whooping was in 7th grade. I lied to my mama about my report card and she waited 'til I got out the shower and busted in the bathroom.

"Were you playing in class or not?" she demanded to know.

"No, ma'am. She just don't like me."

When I said that, she responded with a reflex swing and chopped me across my arm twice.

"Like you? Ain't nobody get paid to damn like you. Don't ever let me hear you say some dumb mess like that." All I had on was a pair of draws and a towel draped over my shoulder.

Yeah, it didn't end well. So, with that image in my mind, I strutted back to class and offered Mrs. Fletcher an apology.

Between the stuff going on at home, the jive with Mrs. Fletcher, and my two-timing girlfriend, I felt like a crushed coke can lying next to the gutter. Then it all came to a head. I was playing volleyball in gym class and spiked the ball extra hard to win a point. I even let out a big yell to show off. Funny though, everybody saw where the ball went, except me. By the time I calmed down from all my gloating, I noticed this big dude in 7th grade walking toward me.

"Hey, yellow-ass nigga, you hit me with the ball. What's up?"

"What, I didn't even know I hit you."

"Yeah, you meant to do that shit." He balled up his hand into a fist.

I backed up. "I would have apologized if I knew I hit you."

Now he was yelling and breathing hard. "Hell with an apology, I'ma see you."

"See me, man...whatever," I said trying to let it go.

Then he ran up to me and pointed toward my face. "Boy, don't walk up on me," I yelled while putting up my hands.

"Dez face is turning red," a girl shouted.

Everybody crowded around, including Kalia, who just happened to be walking by the gym, between classes.

He started to circle around me. "You too little for a fight, but I'ma still whip yo' ass."

"Come with it then." I lunged forward feeling trapped.

My leap of faith led to him grabbing me quicker than I anticipated and we both fell to the floor. He threw two sizzling punches at my face and one hit me in the eye. I threw a punch back but missed. While we were locked up on the ground, I saw Kalia look down and shake her head. Letting him handle me felt like I was even more of a sucker than getting dumped.

"Get 'em, get 'em. Box his ass," people yelled until Coach broke it up.

Coach forced us to shake hands, but he didn't like me and I definitely didn't like him. Sooner or later I knew we would settle it for good.

When he called me, "Yellow" it reminded me of how I had developed toughness for my skin color at a very early age. I owed that to Rich. I could recall numerous times growing up when my brother would say stuff like, "Nigga, you a mayonnaise baby, look at you. You're all light skinned up. You know mama found you on the train tracks. You not even her real child, and you don't look like nobody in our family."

Words like those hurt. Growing up, you had to deal with everything that comes at you or get rolled over. From girls to school, to family and friends, to everything you could imagine. Even at 14, I believed this was true for all people and especially true in the black community. Hurt people hurt others and I had plenty of growing pains to go through.

CHAPTER 16

PAPER THIN

"When you say you love me, it doesn't matter. It goes into my head as just chit chatter. You may think its egotistical or just very free. But what you say, I take none of it seriously."

-MC Lyte

Early March 1990

The weatherman said it was going to be a gorgeous spring day, but black clouds had formed over my school. I was a wanted man and it was only a matter of time before I would be apprehended. "Hold up, this isn't my report card. This ain't got nothing but D's on it," my friend, Ron said aloud as he looked over at me in homeroom.

We had the same last name so sometimes our teacher would hand us the wrong papers by accident.

I knew it had been a mistake when I saw the A's on mine. It was no way I had done anything close to passing. Now, passing out from all the stress lately, maybe...

"Hey Dez, here you go." Ron laughed, handing me my death sentence. His face looked like someone farted on it. "You couldn't pay me to take that home."

I did my best Japanese tourist imitation so that he could barely understand that I was saying thanks.

After getting my card, my mind could not escape the looming punishment. By the time the bell rang in Science class, it was on to lunch and a break from my troubles.

In the cafeteria, Malik stood up and pretended to shoot a basketball. "What y'all think about the Final Four? The tournament's been crazy so far."

"Two words," Jay said being a big Duke fan, "Hill and Laettner."

"Please, they ain't got a chance," I blurted out while almost choking on my pizza. "The Running Rebs 'bout to take it."

"Listen, bruh, Duke plays team ball, them boys at LV ain't ready for that."

"Hold up, why y'all not going for the 'Lethal Weapon Three?'" Malik asked, referring to Georgia Tech's trio of Kenny Anderson, Dennis Scott, and Brian Oliver.

Jay thought about it. "Nah, I kind of like Arkansas, you know they got a black coach, but I can't go against the Dukies, bruh,"

"Okay forget basketball for a sec; y'all seen that En Vogue video?" Malik asked.

"Oh, you talkin' 'bout them girls singing in those black dresses? Good god, they fine," Jay acknowledged. "Yeah Dez, you should have held on to your love, man. You haven't been the same since..." Then he hesitated.

"Nah, you right man, I still can't shake Kalia. Every time I see her in the hall my stomach flips."

"Well flip this. I heard her tell this girl in my class you got beat up before Coach stopped it and she kind of laughed."

My eyes got big as the moon. "For real?"

"For real, and while I'm listening, I'm thinking about how you rode all the way to the mall for that bracelet."

Jay looked like he was watching the plot to movie unfold. "Hey, you still never said why y'all broke up."

I put my head down in my hands. "It's complicated."

Malik jumped all over me. "Man, that's what you said when I asked you about Briana."

"Briana...how did I miss that update?" Jay wondered out loud.

I picked my head up to look at Malik before throwing my report card on the table. He noticed I was upset and paused for a moment. "Yeah Jay, he used to like Briana before Kalia..." Then he spotted the D's on my report card. "Hold up, are those your grades? Oh yeah, Ms. Betty gon' trip."

"Tell me about it." I exhaled and rested my head back in my hands.

"How's yours lookin', Jay Smooth?" Malik asked.

"I got all A's and one B."

"Mr. Engineer always does good. You be at home making love to them books, huh?"

Jay busted out, "You wish."

"Well, what about you?" I asked Malik, hoping to find some company for my misery.

"Nah, not all A's; but its way better than yours."

After a botched forgery attempt on the bus when I tried to turn my 4 D's into B's, I had no choice but to show my mom. She went off like a siren on top of an ambulance.

"What the hell is this? D's…when you started getting D's? All I hear you talk about lately is clothes and music. And then you be sneaking on the phone all time of night. Go call your daddy right now."

After reading my report card to him line by line, he breathed real heavy, and then started his lecture.

"Do I need to come to Savannah? You know how I feel about education. School is important; how the heck you get a D in English?"

"I don't know, Pops."

"Well, don't get any more. I mean *ever*. And you can forget me sending you money for some new shoes."

Okay, how could I respond? I thought English was *boring* as hell. I would be in class dreaming about sleeping or writing rhymes every chance I got. *Why do I have to learn how to talk? I already know how to talk. And who picks these books we have to read and write about?* I knew I couldn't say that, so I swallowed what he had to say and said, "Yes, sir."

In the end, thanks to my laziness and bad attitude, I earned myself some substantial time on punishment. No phone, no Nintendo, and no going outside after school. My once upon a time year had truly hit a brick wall.

A week or so of torture (punishment) had passed, I was in my cell on a Saturday night. I was bored and decided to watch NBC's Saturday night lineup. This consisted of the shows *227, Golden Girls, Amen*, and even *Empty Nest* all back-to-back. I was 14, watching a show starring a group of old fogy white women. They were funny as hell though, and Sophia was my girl.

Anyway, I began to think about the rest of the conversation I had with my dad.

"Dez," he had started, "do you remember me asking if would like to spend next school year in Alabama?"

"Yeah..."

"Well, what do you think?"

At first, I wasn't sure how I felt about it. I hadn't ever been away from Savannah for that long and I wondered how it would feel to go to school in Alabama. I told him I would think about it, but to be honest, I was more concerned about getting off punishment and getting a new girl.

After a few weeks and some good reports from my teachers, I was finally free. To celebrate, I played video games and blasted one of my favorite albums, N.W.A.'s *Straight Outta Compton.*

You would have thought I lived in Compton the way I walked around my room holding my nuts. I played the third song on side two, "A Bitch is a Bitch," over and over until I learned the words by heart. That song made me feel great.

"Okay, hoes can't be trusted, and you know what? I'm 'posed to be mackin' they ass anyway."

I had to be bold. I had to be daring. I had to play the game like a "G", if I was going to rebound from Kalia.

Now, who better to holler at than the girl Jasmine called at the beginning of the year: Shanel. Shanel was a cutie. She had a nice dark skin tone and that "good" straight hair with a dynamite smile that made her desirable. She grew up in Carver Village and had two gold teeth, which I thought was sexy.

"Hey, I'm thinking about talking to Shanel," I told Jay as we walked up the hall.

"Kalia, Briana, Shanel… I can't keep up," he joked. "I don't know Dez, word around school is that she talks to three different dudes and nobody got that game for her. I heard she used to date that drug dealer, Lil Ant out in Liberty City, too."

"Well, I ain't got no dope money," I responded. "All I got is this five dollars for lunch every week."

"You 'bout to give that up?"

"Hell no, I gotta draw the line somewhere."

He busted out laughing. "Hey, there she goes. What's up?"

I patted my hair a couple times and threw a stick of gum in my mouth as I walked up to her.

"Hey Shanel, you gon' speak today or you too good for us regular folks?"

She cut her eyes at me so hard, I had to check if my neck was bleeding. "See here, boy, be quiet…"

"Damn, I can't believe I had a crush on you. Girls like you are not my style."

"Your style?" She almost choked. "Boy, you wish you could pull me."

That stung a bit.

I gotta be bold, I gotta be bold…I coached myself up. *Was she a tease? How could one girl be talking to so many guys at once?*

"So, what are you getting into Friday?"

She closed the magazine she was looking at. "I'm going to the St. Patrick's Day parade with my sister."

"Wow, I ain't been there in a minute. I remember painting my face green and running around like a lil' leprechaun in elementary school," I said.

"They made y'all dress up like leprechauns?"

160

"Yep, you know everybody who's black in Savannah swear they're Irish on the seventeenth."

She laughed then I held out my hand.

"What time are you coming to pick me up so I can go?"

"Boy, I'm too much woman for you," she said walking in class.

I guess I could have kept pressing, but I knew for her, everything was a game.

****

Knowing that I couldn't reel Shanel in, I decided to circle back the girl who I should have chose all along, Briana.

What if I wrote her a letter? Should I come clean and admit that I had messed up earlier in the year? Or maybe I should act like I hadn't done anything at all. When I spotted her at lunch, she was chillin' up against the wall talking to a friend. She looked as cute as ever with her flipped up bucket hat on.

Now was the perfect time to apologize. Yet, the closer I got the more I wanted to keep walking. Getting rejected by Shanel didn't matter one bit. It was just fun. Briana on the other hand was a dream I held on to. I could write 100 raps, but I couldn't say what I wanted to say, to this one girl. Giving her the letter would be perfect, so I quickly dug in my pocket where it was supposed to be, but it had vanished. I panicked and scoped the lunch field for a clue. This was a note no one needed to read but her.

"Is everything okay?" Briana asked.

"Nah, I was just thinking about something." I kept looking around.

She followed my eyes. "So, do you want to share?"

I was about to blow it again until my cousin, Marcus walked up and saved the day.

"Old punk ass, Dez," he called out and laughed.

"Hey Briana, let me see what this fool talking 'bout." I ran over to rush him like I wanted to wrestle. "What are you doing on this lunch?"

He pulled his headphones off. "Man, I'm on every lunch. I see you hollering at that redbone over there." He stared at Briana. "That's you?"

"Nah," I waved his suggestion off. "She's just my friend."

"Your friend? Boy, you stay talking to them good girls, I done told you where that gets you," he huffed.

"How do you know she's a good girl?" I asked. I hated when he was right.

"Well if you don't want to talk to her, I will." He pushed me out of the way.

I grabbed his arm, "She's all wrong for you, you're not her type."

"Oh, she's too good for your own cousin, huh?" He grinned, "Watch this."

My first reaction was to tackle him.

I looked at them talk and talk. She laughed. He laughed. *How could she give him some play?* The wait to see what happened next was killing me. Then she hugged him and I almost lost it.

When he came back over, he looked at me and laughed.

"You alright," he asked.

"Did you get her number?"

"Nah man, that girl likes you. I could tell when I mentioned your name." My jaw dropped.

"You for real, what did she say?"

"Well, I kind of told her you like boys now, Dez-a-ree."

"What?"

Man, I chased that fool all over the field. Finally, I figured he was pro'lly lying and I stopped to catch my breath. The note I had written for Briana fell out my jacket slightly mashed. *Dag... what am I doing?* Then the bell rang.

CHAPTER 17

KEEP ON MOVING

> *"Keep on moving.*
> *Don't stop like the hands of time.*
> *Click clock, find your own way to stay.*
> *The time will come one day.*
> *Why do people choose to live their lives...this way?"*

> **-Soul II Soul**

Late March 1990

The sunset had a yellowish glow and the streetlights were welcoming the night. "Damn, I'm 'bout to be late." I panicked, riding my bike from Head and Jay's house. "I gotta' beat my mama home."

Going there always served as a break from my neighborhood and neither one of them gave me a hard time about crying after the party. I was pedaling so fast that I almost flew over the handlebars just before I bumped into Jarvis.

He was outside washing his mom's car. "Dag, where you coming from, Superman?" He laughed at how I was riding.

I gasped for air. "Jay's."

"Bruh, you ain't came to do no music yet. I thought you were serious?"

"Nah, I'm coming, but right now I need to get home or it won't be nothin' left of me to do anything."

"I hear that. All right, peace, then."

When I pulled up and saw her car in the driveway, I immediately felt nauseous. *Uh oh, this could be ugly.*

At first, when I went in, I didn't hear a thing. I crept inside and I heard their room explode. They were engaged in verbal warfare and the faint trace of liquor I smelt had ignited it.

"I'm sorry. I can't take it no more. *Nigger, you're crazy* if you think I'm going to stand here and keep arguing with you," my mom yelled and pulled a suitcase out of the hall closet.

Okay, this was way worse than getting in trouble for being late. I poked my head back out into the hallway and my mom was on her way out the door before she decided to stop.

"Look here, Dez, I'm staying somewhere else tonight. Tomorrow I'm going to take you to stay in Liberty City. Don't worry. I'm all right. I just have to go."

She stormed out of the front door while my stepdad gave chase in his underwear.

"Betty, Betty," he pleaded, but she wouldn't stop for nothing.

Some of our neighbors heard all the noise and wondered if they should call the police. It didn't take long for her to crank the car and pull off, but then he let the devil fool him. Against all common sense, he darted from the front door and began chasing her car down the street in his underwear and flip-flops until he almost slipped. When he did come back, he was sweating and his flip-flops had magically turned into a set of hooves and a tail. *What a jackass.*

He was in disbelief. He stood in the front door and stared outside for a while. Then, he walked down the hallway and let out one big deep breath. "Damn, I'm tired."

"Shoot, I know you are," I said, while laughing inside.

I wanted to be mad at him for drinking and acting stupid, but at the same time, I felt a little sorry for him. Anything that could make you act like that must be hell to go through. Sheesh. I thought I had some issues; I didn't have nothin' on them.

When he looked at me, I shook my head and sat down to play my video games. I knew that "love" wasn't worth all that fighting and fussing. Finally, I flipped over the Soul II Soul tape I was listening to and fell asleep with Liberty City on my mind.

The next day after school, my mom drove me there to stay with my cousin, Marcus. Before exiting the car, she grabbed my hand to talk. "Look, it's only temporary and I need you to be on your best behavior."

Yeah, it was supposed to be temporary, but my brief stay turned into a months-long journey that changed the way I saw things at 14, forever.

FLICTED

My Aunt Shelia was a lot more relaxed with rules than my mother. She had a laid-back attitude that conveyed "boys will be boys," so as long as we came back in one piece, we were good.

In my eyes, my aunt was the cool mom. When we played cops and robbers as kids, we could always run around her house with toy guns and shoot each other up to have fun. With my mom, you couldn't even make sounds like you had a gun. She had a billion rules. And one rule she stood by was her policy on toy guns. Her only brother had been killed during a gunfight and anytime I asked for a gun, she would say that playing with a gun was practice for killing people.

I thought she was lame for that, and that she just wanted me to be a mama's boy. So I still snuck and played with BB guns whenever I was at Marcus' house. It just seemed like it was a part of being a boy at ten, but now we were teenagers and life was totally different.

"You 'bout to stay with us 'til when?" Marcus asked when I walked in his room.

"I'm not sure. Maybe a week or so."

While he was excited, I was worried about fitting in. Being in a new part of town with new rules was challenging. Everything was new and it was hard to predict. After the ten-minute ride home from school, we hit the neighborhood block every day. In fact, I came on a Wednesday and by the weekend, things had already started jumping off.

That first Saturday night, after everybody in the house was good and asleep, Marcus came in the room with a set of car keys. "Hey, Dez, look, I'ma drive my brother's car 'round the corner to see my girl."

"'Round the corner? Hold up, nigga, are you out your rabbity-ass mind?" I yawned and tried to go back to sleep.

Now his eyebrows were touching and he looked serious. "Nah, she lives in Tatemville. It ain't far, and quit being so scary."

Well, no shit. Why wouldn't I be scared?

After my initial hesitation and pressure from him, I decided to go. When I opened the door and slid in the passenger seat, I kept quietly repeating, "Okay, he knows how to drive. He knows how to drive. He knows…how bad could it be?"

While I thought about everything that could happen, my cousin backed the car out and pulled off like a pro. He didn't even blink. Five minutes later, we arrived at his girlfriend's house, and he hopped out ready for action. His hands were on her waist and his eyes were glued to her lips as they talked on the porch. Finally, he came back to the car, "I'm 'bout to get some. Wait in the car and lookout for her mama," he whispered.

"Her mama…bruh, what the heck I'm 'posed to do if she pulls up? Say, 'Hi?'"

Before we could take it to a vote, he left to go inside. About twenty minutes later while I was sweating bullets in the pitch dark, he came back smiling. He adjusted his belt, then got into the car with one of the funkiest odors I had ever encountered.

I took another whiff and freaked out. "Man, what the hell is that?"

He cranked up the car. "What's what?"

"That smell," I said real slow like I might faint.

"Cuz," he looked me up and down, "that's manhood."

"Well, you need to wash it then, manhood stinks."

I was stuck in disbelief. We had taken the car and he had sex with a girl. I wasn't ready to try this newfound bravery at my own house, but while I stayed with Marcus, sneaking out occurred regularly.

That Monday in the hallway at school, I leaned up against the wall with Malik before class started.

"Bruh, my cousin is wild as hell," I said, after finishing most of the story.

"Man, you better be careful out there. You know Ol' Betty will kill you," Malik laughed at my crazy adventure.

"Yeah, I know. But it might have been worth it, bruh; his girl is sooo fine."

"What his girl got do with you, though?" he asked.

"Man, let me finish the story." I pretended to slap him.

But then Marcus walked up. He tapped me on the shoulder and reached into his book bag. "Dez, I need you to hold these for me and take 'em on the bus."

"Joker, hold your own books. I ain't no do-boy."

He looked up and down the hallway. "Nah, clown, it ain't like that. I got something to do. I'm serious, look out for me."

I reluctantly took his books and made my way to class. No sooner than I had stepped in, the principal came over the intercom. "Teachers, lock your doors the police are conducting a search for drugs and weapons. There is absolutely no movement," she said.

Lucky me, I wound up in Mr. Cook's boring English class.

I had almost fallen asleep when my foot kicked one of the books Marcus had given me onto the floor. I looked down to pick it up and as plain as day, a fat marijuana joint was on the ground next to it.

Man, it might as well have been crack that fell out of that book because I was petrified. I looked to see if anyone was paying attention and then I quickly put the joint back into the book and closed it. I didn't know what to do. The whole time, I prayed the police didn't come to my class. If they had, I probably would have pissed on myself. I was that scared.

When Marcus got home that afternoon, I was in his room waiting. I threw the book on his bed in front of him and stared at it for a while. Then I exploded, "Bruh, don't ever do no dumb shit like that."

He smirked. "Dag, ain't like you got caught. Chill out."

"But I could have got caught." I punched him in the arm.

"You wouldn't have gotten caught, 'cause they not looking for an honor roll student. They were looking for me."

"Man, whatever, that's some bull."

"All right, then let's go," he said, real slick and pushed me on the bed.

I knew he let me win on purpose because I had never handled him that easy. After I pinned him down, he actually started laughing. "Look, walk to the store with me. I'll pay for whatever you want. Everything cool?"

Marcus had bought into street life from watching his older dudes in the neighborhood hustle, and you could tell that he loved it.

On the way up the street, some older dudes were booming "Roll It Up My Nigga" by Success-n-Effect out of a parked Monte Carlo.

FLICTED

We were soaking up the scene, when my cousin's best friend, Reggie, "Big Reg," came around the corner shouting along with the lyrics, "I'm with it. I'm with it." He jumped around like he was high.

Big Reg was tall as hell, and looked like he should have been in somebody's high school, yet he was only in the 7th grade.

Marcus grinned and pulled out a joint to hit. "Reg is crazy, he got a dude 'round the corner scared to come outside over two dollars."

"Two dollars, for real?" I asked.

"Yeah he ain't gon' fight him, though. He don't fight people that he knows he can beat 'less they really did something."

"Shoot, I saw him fight two dudes from Beach High at the same time last month," I recalled as I watched him continue to dance.

Marcus nodded. "Yeah, everybody was talking about that for weeks."

"How long have you all known each other?"

"Since the third grade when we started a group called the Ditch boys."

I laughed. "I remember that. Y'all used to jump out by the sewer and wrestle people walking to the store."

"Yep that was us all day." Marcus reached out to dap Reg up. "Anybody who tried to jump on me, that man has always been there to help." Reg threw a slow motion punch at me so I had time to duck.

"'Sup Dez, don't let your cousin tell you lies 'bout I'm crazy. He's the one influencing me." Then he and Marcus started to trade punches until Marcus ran. "People think I'm crazy, I peep everything, though. It's like this song on the radio, everybody think it's telling folks to smoke weed, but if you listen, they really telling you not to."

Marcus looked at him funny. "Nigga, but you still smoke."

"I know, but shit, least I know not to." He laughed.

I got to know Reg well while I was in Liberty City and something crazy was always happening when I hung out with him and Marcus.

Late that Friday evening, we were at my cousin's house doing much of nothing. They were talking about some freaky girls in the neighborhood while we sat around watching videos on The Box.

"Man, they play the same damn video over and over," Reg said, like he was exhausted.

Marcus shouted across the room, "Request something then."

"I ain't paying no two-ninety-nine for a video. I'll wait."

I agreed with Reg. "Man, I been waiting all day to see 'Flavor of the Month' but they keep playing 'B Girls'."

Reg began shuffling a deck of cards. "Hey Dez, let me teach you how to play Tonk so I can take all your lunch money."

"Uh oh, this my part y'all." I sang along.

"B stands for, Broncos, Benz, BMW, bass, bangles and a pair of bars. When you see us pulling up down the Ave, you'll act like we are stars."

"You like this song, Dez?" Reg asked.

"Yeah, you can't help but like it when they play it so much."

Once Big Reg taught me the basic rules of Tonk, I was hooked.

I easily won the first few games and stood up to boast.

"Hold up, that's three in a row and I doubled out, so you owe me five dollars."

"Man, let's finish this bullshit later," Reg said, standing up. Then, he threw the cards on the table and let out a nasty yawn like he hadn't slept in days. "Bruh, I might be hungraaay. Let's get some pizza."

"I could go for that." Marcus patted his stomach.

We had three dollars between us and that wasn't nearly enough money.

"I tell you what," Reg leaned in and said to my cousin, "let's call the pizza man to that empty house 'round the corner and rob his ass."

I immediately thought, *Rob? Man, y'all tripping.* But before I knew it, they were gone.

About an hour or so later, Marcus and Reg came bursting through the door laughing with two hot pizzas. Grease and cheese was hanging off their hands. After they set the boxes down, we tore through what was left.

I didn't ask any questions. I just ate.

Seeing a rap I wrote on the table, Big Reg cleared his throat. "Dez, you be trying to rap, huh?"

"A lil' something."

"Wow." He was genuinely surprised. "That's cool. Who you rap like, De La Soul and them? I bet you didn't think I knew about them."

"Nah, I know you hip." I dapped him up. "I like De La...but I pro'lly rap more like Kane or EPMD."

Reg put a two-liter to his mouth and drank the last swallow of soda. "What you know 'bout the Geto Boys?" he asked.

"Nah, I ain't heard of them. Where they from?"

"Houston, you should check them out." He pulled out a sack of weed and gave it to my cousin. "Them boys be spittin' that real shit."

Marcus agreed, "I hope you got better, Dez, 'cause you used to be embarrassing."

I jumped out of my chair for an answer. "Embarrassing when?"

"C'mon now, I still remember how you used to beg to go to the store on 52nd Street that had that big jukebox." He politely pushed me back into the chair. "Reg, this fool Derrick would put money in the box and rap over all the songs."

"You remember all that? Dag. Well, yeah, I'm better now. We were like nine years old then."

Now Reg was intrigued. "Let me hear what's on your paper."

I hit a quick beat box then stopped. "I need a beat, though."

"I can't do all that beat boxin', spittin' stuff." Reg waved his hands. "But I can bam on the table and make something."

He started with a nice easy 1-2 rhythm that got heavy the more he bopped his head to it. Boom bap, Boom bap, Boom Boom. Boom bap, Boom bap, Boom Boom.

Don't mess up. This is your chance to show 'em. I had already memorized my lines so I was ready.

Young poet,
with the mic in my hand.

174

FLICTED

Turn the flesh on ya body
into nothin but sand.
When my fire ignites
I blind with the light.
Sunshine ain't enough,
know I'm twice as bright.
From Savannah, And I... plan to set it off.
Call 'em to a battle
them boys won't even cough.
No way, no how, better learn whatcha' doin'
Super rap flow, look I ain't even human."

Reg went crazy. "Oh shit Dez, you got them I dare you to rap against my rhymes. I'ma tell you though, you need to write some stuff about having fun, too; that's how you get on the radio for them parties."

Marcus looked like he was proud for a quick sec. "Yeah, you got a lot better, man."

Everything in Liberty City was just fine, until we hit the block.

CHAPTER 18

SCARFACE

> *"I started small time, dope game, cocaine. Pushin' rocks on the block, I'm never broke, mayne sportin' jewelry and shit that came with rolling hard. You try to school me, you'll get fucked with no regard."*

-Geto Boys

Early April 1990

Darkness swooped down on the streets of Savannah's Westside. While many people went to sleep for the next day, others were just getting started. The night I hung out with my cousin on "the block," everything changed. This wasn't just any block. It was one of the main streets in Liberty City where everybody and their mama came through to buy drugs, boosted clothes, and whatever else they needed.

FLICTED

A dude named Wah-wah posted on the corner, stared at me as we walked up. "Hey Marcus, who lil' man is? He looks like he should be home getting tucked in bed."

Everyone on the block laughed. *Why I gotta be getting tucked in bed?*

"Nah, that's my cousin, Dez." Marcus paused to look at me. "Don't worry, he's cool."

That night they introduced me to some older guys who fronted younger cats drugs to sell. Some had fathers in the dope game; so for them, selling dope was a way of life. I didn't know how large those operations were, but I remembered the scenes of glowing porch lights and people walking up to buy stuff. Dudes would reach into their pocket like magicians, make an exchange, and then fiends would disappear.

That night, they were huddled on the corner like the opening drive of a football game, and the play was, "I got 'dizzum' to sell."

At first, I was a fan; excitement was there, and I liked being out late. Different than the Southside, it made me feel harder being out in the streets.

I was leaning up against a stop sign talking to my cousin when a gray van pulled up.

A white dude in the passenger side poked his head out the window like he was feindin'.

"Hey bros, we wanna score some dope."

Seizing the moment, Big Reg walked toward the ride. "Ain't nobody got no dope, cracker. Give me all your money and haul ass 'fore I shoot you." Then he pointed a shotgun at the driver's head. Both of the people in the car immediately put their hands up.

"Please don't shoot us...I'll give you what I got." The passenger was shaking like a pair of dice in a hot hand, but he still managed to take out almost eighty dollars' worth of crumbled up bills.

Reg smiled, then hit the top of the car like a brick. "Speed on and don't come back on my block."

I didn't know what to say. I might have seen something like that on TV but never in front of my face. People on the block looked up when it happened, but nobody said a word. On the way home that night, my cousin laughed about it.

He took a hit of a joint and held it out for me. "Hey, Reg crazy, right?"

"Come on, you know I don't smoke." I knocked his hand away. "Where that man get a gun from?" I didn't expect an answer and he didn't give one.

I had love for them boys, but seeing that go down, I knew I wasn't built for the block.

****

"Why aren't you out there with Marcus and his friends?" my mom asked, after she stopped by one day to check on me.

It's not like I could say, *"Hey, ya' know what? Marcus kinda sells dope."* Or even better, *"How many fourteen year-olds you know own a shotgun?"*

So instead, the conversation went something like this:

"I thought you loved hanging with Marcus, why you not outside?"

"Oh, I got a lot to do. And you know Marcus doesn't do homework, so…"

My mom smiled, nodded, then paused for a while.

FLICTED

"You know, I wasn't sure how you would handle staying out here, but I'm glad you're not afraid to separate yourself. I always tell you to watch your friends, 'cause everybody who say that they're for you, ain't for you."

The more I chilled, the more focused I became. I'd knock out my homework, then sit on the porch to practice. I would listen to all the tapes that my cousin's big brother had for inspiration. Albums like Cool C, Tuff Crew, and Queen Latifah's first release were lying around the house like dirty dishes that nobody wanted to touch, except me.

Writing was all I did after school until Marcus started looking at me funny and asking questions.

"How do you sit and write all day? I thought rappers made money. You can't make money sitting round the house."

"Nah, I'm practicing." I laughed.

He took off his Polo and squeezed his head inside of a T-shirt to wear outside. "Well, let some folks hear it; don't you need fans?"

Now, he was right about that, I thought.

"I be hearing you outside freestyling. You don't sound half bad, but you gotta stop with them fake-ass interviews."

I lay back on the bed and folded my hands behind my head. "Half bad, c'mon man…that's it?"

He pretended to drop his elbow on me. "Look, if you believe in yourself, keep doing it. I'm just saying don't let your heart pump Kool Aid."

I touched my heart and chuckled. "Hey cuz, why you go on the block every day?" I obviously didn't understand his decisions. "Your parents got bread."

"For money," he said. "My parents' money ain't mine. And to be honest, I like being in the middle of shit.

179

Staying in the house all up in some books...that shit is boring."

"You know my mom asked me if you were off?" he said, switching the conversation back to me.

I looked at him like he was speaking Chinese. "Off?"

"Yeah, she saw you on the porch mumbling. I told her you call yourself rapping and that I thought you were alright even though I'm not really sure." He laughed.

"So, you staying in today? I'm fin hit the block."

I threw a pair of balled up socks at him. "Nah, I'm good, cuz. I gotta work if I'm going to be a famous rapper."

Maybe I was crazy to dream the way I did, but I wanted much more out of life than the block. Ironically, while I had all the freedom I wanted, my grades improved, too. This was definitely true in Mrs. Fletcher's class. That Friday when I saw her in the hall she told me she had some big news. When I sat down in class I didn't know what to expect.

"Okay everyone, the grades for the fair came back." She smiled and wiggled her shoulders in excitement.

"You all did a great job. First place went to someone in another class but we had the second and third place winners."

Is she crazy, she stopped me in the hall like I would be excited about this – give me a break...

"Second place was Kate Fleming who did an amazing job."

Everyone clapped and yelled out congratulations.

Then, she said, "And, third place was our own scholar, Mr. Derrick Allen."

When the last syllable leaped out, everyone's mouth opened in shock.

"You paid the judges off," Angela said, like there was no other possible explanation.

Ms. Fletcher continued, "Again, thank you all for working so hard and showing the school you are the leaders of tomorrow. Today, I want your help in starting our video project."

"What it's about?" I asked as she now had my attention.

"Well, I want you to use your talents to talk about drugs and violence. You can make posters, come up with skits, and use any other thing you can think of to inspire your peers to make positive choices."

Everyone was enthused. She pulled out her camera and we thought we were stars.

"And, I want my two rap artists, Angela and Derrick, to do a special rap for it."

Cool, it was definitely time to show what I could do... Ol' Fletcher was cool after all.

By the end of the week, I was rapping and dancing with Angela (Lo-lo) for the project and it came out great. She told us to keep it up and that made me feel like I had accomplished something big.

I came home that Friday afternoon, ready to tell Marcus about the rap we made, but before I could get it out, he had something a bit more exciting to share.

"Guess what, we're going to the skating rink tonight. You coming?"

I had never been to the Eastside skating rink, but in my eyes... it was legendary.

In an instant, I was transported back to my summer in Alabama and all the fun I had watching girls dance. We talked up a ride from one of Reg's cousins who lived in Housing Project called Garden Homes, but by the time he dropped us off, we were late. The lines were super long. It was so many people. They would only let one person in when another person came out.

"Man, let's go. We'll mess 'round and be out here all night," Reg said.

I wanted to get in bad. "C'mon. Let's try to wait."

Marcus had already lost his patience. "Bruh, you see that line? I saw all the females when they went in, so ain't really no point, 'less you bout to holla."

Before I could respond, Big Reg cut in, "That line is for the birds. I'm fin to walk to Kroger's and get some food."

And just like that, we left. Posted up in front of the grocery store, I saw a few girls who went to our school pushing each other around the lot in those shopping carts that looked like little buggies.

"Man, them girls look high. What are they doing?" Marcus said, looking to see who it was.

"Hey that's AC and them. Let's see what they talking 'bout." Reg looked at me. "Alright Dez, your lil' red ass should be mackin'. You know their crazy 'bout y'all light skin dudes. All you gotta do is tell 'em what they wanna hear."

He spoke like I had some kind of powers I didn't realize. If they were there, they laid pretty dormant. What would it take for them to come out?

We walked up to them in full flirt mode and began clowning around to have a good time.

First, Marcus and Reg checked each other back and forth, then Reg got me to bust a rap.

AC looked surprised. "Damn Dez, I didn't know you could flow." *Yeah, I could get use to this.*

182

All of a sudden, a hooptie drove through the parking lot blasting music.

You could tell the driver was trying to flex, but the system sounded like junk. Every time the bass would drop, it rattled like the car was falling apart at the hinges. Everyone with us started laughing.

I looked at Marcus. "Hey, he's playing your group, Poison Clan."

"Nigga, turn that raggedy ass shit off," Big Reg shouted.

When he said that, everybody began whooping and hollering with laughter louder than before.

SCREECH. Within seconds, the car stopped and the driver jumped out.

"Which one of y'all lil' niggas said something 'bout my ride?"

Before we could breathe, he pulled out a gun and everybody froze. Slightly moving my eyes, I looked at my cousin. Then he looked at Reggie.

Death was in the air and still Big Reg stuck his chest out. "Nigga, I said it."

Albeit foolish, this was the most impressive form of bravery I had ever seen. He had a loaded weapon in his hand, but Reg would not bow down. A fraction of a second later, as the look of disbelief wore off, the dude took his gun and pistol-whipped Reggie across the face. Blood burst from his mouth and began to skeet like a sprinkler. Then, the guy backed up real slow, maintaining an aim at Reg's chest.

"Pussy-ass nigga," he shouted as he jumped in his car and mashed on the gas to drive away.

Once the guy sped off, Reggie looked at us with his head down for a minute. He spat out some blood to the ground, leaned back on the wall and said, "After tonight, man, I'm never leaving the house without my pistol. Fuck that."

Next, Reg called his cousin's pager, we waited almost an hour, but he finally came and drove us back to Liberty City. I couldn't get it out of my head. First the cops, now a young black man was ready to kill us. Again, we were expendable.

"We can go look for the nigga if you want?" Reg's cousin handed him a pistol after listening to a quick version of the story.

"Yeah, drop Marcus and them off first. Savannah's only so big, we gon' see him eventually."

"Bet, y'all boys want to hit this joint?" Reg's cousin asked as we got on the road.

"Nah, I'm straight tonight. I know my mom will be up waiting on us."

Reg took off his blood-stained shirt and rolled down the window. "I'm fin to hit it 'fore I snap in here."

Once we got in the house, I sat down on the bed to think. My mind was all over the place. *A radio. A damn radio. We could have died over an insult.* I looked over at my cousin and he was asleep, so I woke his ass up.

"Man, what happened doesn't bother you?"

He rolled around a couple times, then sat up. "Look, I don't like that shit but when you out here in the streets, you gotta be careful what you say. Anything can happen." He stretched a bit, then laid back down. "Just imagine if Reg had had his gun."

When he said that, I heard nothing but gunshots in my head.

"Trust me, somebody would have died tonight," he said before rolling over to go back to sleep.

Somehow I knew he was right.

That next day, Reg came over and talked to Marcus about what happened after they dropped us off. There were a few more of their friends with them, so we ordered some pizzas and chilled for a while.

I could tell Reg was still mad, and every now and then he would touch the bruise on his face from the gun.

While we were eating, Marcus started to clean out a shed in the back yard his dad had been asking about, when he stumbled onto his old boxing gloves. "What y'all know 'bout these?"

"Oh shit, who got them hands?" Reg asked as his face lit up.

Marcus tossed Reg the pair of ol' busted up gloves that had seen their fair share of battles.

Once Reg put his pair on, he looked at all their friends and everybody immediately backed up. Finally he looked over at me. "What up, Southside? What you got?"

What I got? I wanted to say I didn't have shit, but I couldn't back down. I knew and everybody else knew I didn't have a chance in hell. Still, I said, "What's up?" and grinned like I had a plan. This earned me a smidgen of respect along with plenty pity from everyone watching.

I felt Big Reg thought I was cool in a different sort of way and wouldn't try to kill me. I psyched myself out and asked, "What's the worst that could happen?"

It was a first-round TKO. I hit the ground three times during the match while running around trying to keep my guard up.

"You can take a punch pretty good," he acknowledged.

"Yeah, that's not exactly something I'd like to be known for," I yelled back.

Seizing the moment, I took a cheap shot at him when he stopped to laugh and that joker chased me around the house for about ten minutes before asking me to stop.

"Hold up, Dez. Man, I gotta teach you how to throw a punch," he said, laughing. "Don't swing too hard with the same hand as the foot you're leading with, it'll throw you off balance."

"What?"

"Listen, you can jab, but don't throw haymakers from that side. Throw your hard punches from the opposite side. And look, don't stand directly in front of who you're fighting. Either turn to the side with your shoulder out or move a bit. Otherwise you're an easy target." And then he pulled Marcus over to show me exactly what he meant.

"Man Reg, don't hit me for real." Marcus flinched.

Actually, it was the first lesson on fighting I had ever had—for him it was nothing. For me it was like *damn, I been doing this wrong my whole life.*

I could see the way drugs and quick cash created a path for them that we didn't have to take on the Southside. If you did take it, I assumed it was something you chose, like Marcus. He didn't have to be out there dealing. He just was. On the other hand, Big Reg seemed like he did what he did to survive. I wasn't sure how much money his family had, but the times we went there to pick him up, they looked like they were about ten deep in a house that was made for four people.

Later that day, after the boxing matches, we were all hanging around the house playing basketball, and everybody, except for me, was high.

"Yeah, them boys from Tatemville think they just gon' jump Lo and Terry," Marcus said, looking at Reg.

186

"Not if I'm around. Why everybody wanna jump somebody these days?" Reg replied. "I'ma put these hands on 'em if they try that."

No one asked me if I was going to help if a fight started, but I could feel that they wanted to know. I wouldn't let anyone jump on my cousin; however, I wasn't planning to fight in an all-out war with another neighborhood, either. They all grew up where they had to fight along with their neighborhood or street. That way if someone tried to fight you from another neighborhood, they had your back as well.

I had never lived with that kind of pressure. If I fought someone it was just Me, Myself, and I. While my mom emphasized staying out of trouble, many of them had been raised with the mantra: *If someone hits you and you don't whip they ass, when you come home, you're gonna get your ass whipped for losing.*

This was a very different mentality to have. Creatures adapt to their environment or perish. So I began to think very deeply...sort of like a philosopher... *if I have to get involved, what would I do?* That answer came quicker than I planned when Marcus looked at me straight up and said, "Hey cuz, I need you to help us fight."

CHAPTER 19

RAW

"Twenty-four sev chillin',
killin' like a villain. The meaning of
R.A.W. is ready and willin' to do
whatever is clever, take a loss
never. And the rhymes I bust,
definitely a must."

- Big Daddy Kane

Mid-April 1990

It was like the finale of an epic movie. Clear turquoise waves splashed against her caramel skin and pretty feet. Then, she called me to lie down beside her. I practically begged her to forgive me. After taking a moment to make me wait, she leaned in for a kiss. Then my alarm went off and my dream about Briana was gone.

"Wake up." Marcus snatched the covers off. "I done called you three times…"

"What… okay…" Then, I dozed off again.

"Alright, pay back," he snickered and left the room.

Next thing I knew, I felt some drops of water. Then, before I could move...BOOSH. I had water all over me.

I shook like a wet dog after a bath. "Man, damn..."

"Look, c'mon 'fore you make us late for the bus," he said. "And, your favorite rapper is on the radio."

"Who?" I scrunched up my face.

He turned up the radio. "Big Daddy Kane's on the radio...listen."

Nah, it can't be. Big Daddy Kane in Savannah? Whoa. That morning, he had been on the radio station promoting a concert he was in town for.

"What's the tour all about?" the host asked Kane.

"We want to inspire the youth and show them there is a better way to handle their problems besides fighting."

The host was impressed. "How did you handle problems when you were young?"

Kane cleared his throat. "Don't get me wrong, I had my share of rumbles. But I had lots of positive influences like my dad and brothers in the Five Percent Nation who taught me to seek wisdom and strive to do the right things."

To hear my favorite rapper talking like that was huge. After that, the host played two of my favorite Kane songs. "Raw" and the "Lean on Me" remix from the movie soundtrack. I could quote both of those songs line for line. We didn't get many concerts, especially outside of the summertime, so when we did have one, it was a *big deal*.

I looked like a bomb had went off when I arrived at school. "Y'all heard Kane on the radio this morning? I'm telling you he's the best rapper alive."

Jay flung his hand toward me. "Nah, nobody is fresher than Slick Rick."

Everybody made their point and, of course, we couldn't agree. Some said it was Slick Rick, other people loved LL Cool J and Rakim. KRS and Ice Cube were hard too, but for me in 1990, it was hands down, Big Daddy Kane.

On the radio, they said he might visit a few high schools to promote stopping black-on-black violence like the song, *Self-Destruction*.

Man, it would be fresh if he came to our school. On the way to third period, it was like someone lit a stick of dynamite and threw it, 'cause the rumors of Kane being at our school made the hallways explode.

Much to my surprise, Big Daddy Kane, along with Ice T, had come and left. I couldn't believe it. How did they choose who got to meet them? No one I knew had a clue about what went down, so I missed out completely.

When I saw Marcus, I asked him if he heard about Kane coming and he looked like he couldn't care less. Instead, he interrupted my excitement with questions about the girl I thought I had gotten completely over.

"Boy, I saw Kalia before we got on the bus. Dag, that girl know she fine. You broke up a while back, right? Man, why?" He didn't wait for me to answer. "I'm surprised y'all even went together."

"Why you say it like that?" I asked, somewhat offended.

"She's not your type. Trust me, I know."

"So, what's my type?" I rolled my eyes.

"Well, not her. You know you ain't trying to do nothing. You probably want to hold hands and cuddle." He began hugging the air.

"Man, forget you."

"Me? I be bustin' these girls dowwwn," he growled.

190

I looked out the window to show my disproval. "And she's that type, 'cause you would know, right?"

"Well, have you had any?" he asked.

When I thought about it, I just went blank. At that age, I didn't feel I could do anything, even if I did think about it all the time. I guess I was scared. Scared of a baby, scared of not knowing what do to, scared of my parents, and scared of *God*.

"Nah, cuz, to be honest…I haven't," I finally replied.

My cousin looked at me. He was in shock. Then, it switched to a look of disgust. "Hold up. How you ain't had none yet?" he asked, his hands covered his face.

I felt the weight of his disbelief and I began to feel somewhat ashamed. I was proud that I thought for myself most of the time, but his look really got to me. After a minute or so, his disgust changed to a look of sorrow. Then he announced that it was his duty to help.

"Hey, Dez, I'm going to look out for you. I know this broad up the street from the house. Bruh, if I give her a rock, she'll let me and you get busy."

Sex for crack?

"You sure, man?"

"Look, this is a grown woman. She's about thirty and fat up. Her body is right." he said.

At that precise moment, a light bulb went off in my head. I could no longer contain my curiosity about sex once Marcus set his plan in motion. Now, it was time for the details of this "great plan."

It was twelve o'clock on a school night when we decided to sneak out the house to where she lived.

As we walked slowly down the hallway, I couldn't help but question what I was doing. Here I was, dumb as ever, following my cousin into who knows what. I guess I wanted to be a real man, and having sex, however I could get it, seemed to be what a real man would do. Right?

We snuck out through the sliding glass door and walked down a dirt road that was more like a lane next to a ditch. It was a remote looking part of Liberty City where folks used to say *Dan the Boonkie Man* lived. This was an urban legend about a crazy man who went around molesting kids. When we got there, Marcus looked around for a minute, then knocked on her door.

"Man, she gotta be here," he said, over and over.

"Let me knock," I offered. I didn't want to seem unappreciative, so I began tapping on the old rickety screen door with a beat.

"Nah, you gon' have to knock harder than that," Marcus said as he went to the side window to look in the house.

"What's up? Is she there?"

"Nah cuz, she's not home. We'll try again soon."

I was relieved that I didn't have to make this my first time, but I didn't want to tell him that.

"I didn't have rubbers anyway." He chuckled. "We would have hit it raw."

"Raw? Damn, I didn't even think about protection…why would we hit it raw?"

"I mean if you have a rubber, then use it. But if not, long as you pull out before you bust, then you straight."

I shivered at the thought. "What about diseases and stuff?"

"I mean she smoke rocks but she clean." He stopped to look at me. "She don't got no diseases, you would be able to tell."

"I don't know, man," I said as we crossed the street.

Just then, the neighbor's dog began barking.

"What the hell," I said looking over my shoulder. "He gon' mess 'round and get us caught."

Marcus started to jog. "Well, walk up, then."

"Oh shit, their gate is open. "I watched as that dog sprinted toward us. "That nigga running over here. Marcus, hurry up."

"Hell, I'm fin to jump." He leaped over the gate.

With no time to spare, I followed suit, minus a safe landing.

Marcus laughed. "Hey, he almost got us. You straight? You look like you're paralyzed."

"I should be, I landed on my head."

We sat in the yard for a second 'til the dog stopped barking, then we snuck back into the house.

God, I was thankful that woman never came to the door that night. I don't know who or what lived in that house we knocked on. Yet, the fact that it could have happened gave me chills for awhile.

With the thought of sex so close, I had changed from wanting to be hunted to being the hunter. Being around Reg and Marcus taught me how to move through the jungle—and I began to develop an appetite.

The first thing I noticed was how differently I looked at Jasmine. She and Malik had been done for months, and I wasn't talking to her on the phone as much as I used to. Then one day that week, I saw her in the hallway, and my instincts kicked in.

"Dag, Jasmine, you look good today, and you got them sexy hairy legs." I followed this up with a slight sexual grunt—a mating call, if you will.

"Boy, stop playing," she said, pushing me away. "Don't play with my emotions. Besides I can't date my best friend." She walked off switching extra hard. My true intention was never to try anything, (or so I would tell myself) but the thought of it was real.

Later in the week, I was walking in the hall with Head when my newly acquired sexual appetite took control again.

"Bruh, you know I had never seen Kwame's video 'til the other night. You saw how good Spinderella looked?" I asked.

"Yeah, I been told you 'bout that video. You know he 'posed to perform with Salt-N-Pepa at Savannah State soon."

"Nah, for real? Bruh, we gotta go. Hey, when you get that?" I pointed at the necklace around his chest. Head was wearing a new African medallion, which, at the time, was a hip-hop status symbol. I had wanted one for the longest, so I asked him if I could hold it.

When he went to take it off, his arm hit this girl named Dion who was walking by.

"Dag, bruh. You 'bout to knock a sistah out," she yelled.

It was funny how things came together. That moment seemed so accidental, yet it was very significant. That day was the first day I really noticed her. Her style, her flavor, her everything was dope. Maybe life in the jungle that was Liberty City, allowed me to detect the pheromones she released.

In a split second, I decided to test my new ability. I waved, then put my hand on her shoulder as I spoke.

"Hey, Dion, you look nice today. When can I call you?"

"Who, me?" she asked, blushing.

She had a surprised look like she had no idea I was that forward. Jasmine, who was standing close by gave her a look that said, "Go head, girl." And Dion blushed again.

Once I knew she was feeling me, I checked her out every chance I got. From afar, like a hunter adjusting the scope on his gun, I patiently waited.

Dion reminded me of Molly Ringwald and Freddie from *A Different World* without all the ditziness.

She was smart, hip, and she had a pretty light brown skin complexion with long wavy hair. She was not typical so I decided to talk to Jasmine about her, wondering if she would object to my new crush.

"Hey, you know I'm feeling your girl, Dion. I'm going to call her and see what she talking 'bout."

"What? Look at you, Derrick," Jasmine said, as if she was proud of my newfound confidence. "You done *growed* up on me. I'm blushing." Then, she pretended to wipe away her fake tears.

"Whatever."

"Nah, she's cool, you should call her."

The next day when I got ready to call Dion, I did the exact same thing I did when I called Kalia for the first time. I wasn't at home, but I made sure the coast was clear and I went to call Dion from my aunt's bedroom. I rehearsed a couple lines, then, I took my shoes off and propped myself up in Aunt Shelia's bed to make the call.

When Dion answered, her voice was warm and sultry. It was like she had another gear, and I had no idea of how it worked. I expected someone that was super polite and coy, but she was hip and laid back like I was talking to a homeboy. We talked for maybe five minutes and I decided to play my hand.

"Look, Dion, I like you. I think you're cute and," I paused for dramatic effect, "I want to be your man."

"I don't know what to say," she admitted.

"I want to go with you, so… just say you want to be my girl."

"Okay, yes…I want to."

It was all so fast and easy that it felt a bit strange. I tell you, confidence is something else. I didn't really know her at all, but Dion was about to show me a whole other side of love.

CHAPTER 20

SOMEBODY FOR ME

"Now maybe I'll take a trip around the world and find myself a beautiful, gorgeous girl. They say when you look, one never finds. They also say that love is blind."

-Heavy D and The Boyz

Late April 1990

In the beginning, going with Dion was like being resurrected from the dead. She breathed life into my school year and I was ready to be her man. She was well known around school and everybody quickly found out that we were an item. Having a girlfriend was quite an accomplishment. Dudes gave me respect for going with her and a lot of girls around school said we made a cute couple. From the get-go, I walked her to class, we talked on the phone, and she wrote me lots of notes that made me feel special.

Everything was gravy until Dion called me after we had been together for two weeks.

"Hey, I don't like that you and Jasmine are so close. What's up with that? I think she like you or something."

"Huh? What are you talking about? I thought y'all were cool?"

"We *used* to be cool like that," she snapped off.

All the "prissy white girl" smoke screen she had been working, disappeared. Now, I heard that *straight up west side sass.*

"Chill, Jasmine is like my sister."

"Whatever." She sucked her teeth to make sure I heard it. "I know when skeezers are up to something."

Since I started going with Dion, Jasmine was acting different. Not bad, just different, and I didn't know why. *Hadn't she co-signed Dion back in the hallway and on the phone?* Any ol' way, other than the weirdness with Jasmine, going with Dion was straight. I talked with her more than I had with Kalia, and I was able to be myself, which was great.

Unexpectedly, the next day during third period, the principal called me to the office. I didn't know what to think. My mind raced to everything I had done in the past week to make sure I wasn't walking into some sort of trap. I kept thinking hard, but I had no idea what was what until I walked in and saw my stepdad talking with Principal McKane like two old friends.

"Wow, so this is your stepson?" she said.

My stepdad rubbed me on my head. "Yes, this is Derrick, but everyone calls him Dez."

"I haven't had any problems out of him. Looks like he's in all honors classes, too," the principal said, seeming impressed. "How's the year going, young man? How are your grades?" she asked.

"Uhhh...it could be better, but my grades have been improving lately." *That was one good thing about being in Liberty City. Now, imagine me telling them about sneaking out and the pizza robbery.*

"Okay, I'll let you two talk," my principal said and walked out of the office.

My stepdad cut right to it. "Hey, I haven't seen or spoken with your mama in weeks. Where are y'all living at?" he demanded.

"I'm in Liberty City," I said, not realizing it was top secret.

"And your mom?"

"Uhhh..."

There was a long, awkward pause before he finally said, "Look tell her to call me," then he gave me a hug and walked out.

Feeling bothered, I left the office, blew out a deep sigh, and thought about home. I hadn't been there in almost a month. I wasn't itching to go back just yet, but I did miss it. As I walked back to class, the breezeways were empty so I ran my hand along the side of the building, trying to think. *What would Alabama be like for ninth grade?*

I needed to talk to someone. I just didn't know who or how.

I had wasted another few minutes walking in the hall, when I bumped into Dion and one of her friends.

"What are you doing out here?" she asked, leaning toward me for a hug.

"Nothing, I went to use the bathroom and was in the hall wasting time."

"Girl, we better get back to class before the bell." Her friend looked around.

"Hey, Dez, is Mya in your class this period?" Dion asked.

"Yeah, what's up?"

She reached out for my hand. "Do me a favor and give her this note for me."

Thinking that I was being a good boyfriend, I took the note, gave her another hug, and said goodbye. For some reason, I remember her friend shaking her head. I didn't know why, but it made me feel like I had missed a joke or something.

I was almost at my English class when I decided to be nosey and open the letter Dion had given me for Mya. I just knew she had something good to say about us. She was probably going to mention how good looking I was or how funny... *No, I know*...she was going to talk about how fresh I dressed. Man, I was grinning like a full fat man after Thanksgiving when I opened that letter.

In the beginning, it was the usual girl stuff:

Hey, Girl, what's up? Class is boring as a mug, so I decided to write you a note.

It wasn't anything special ...*until* I saw my name. At that point, my emotions shot up in the air. I thought she was about to say how much she really liked me. But I was *very, very, very wrong.* Instead of singing my praises, the note put me on notice.

Girl, I like Dez, and these last couple weeks have been pretty good but last night my old boyfriend, Cedric called me and asked me to go back with him.

FLICTED

Now you know, I couldn't pass his fine ass up, so I said yes. Girl o' Girl, what should I do?

What should you do? How 'bout, **not** give your new boyfriend this damn note.

My pride was very hurt, though I took it on the chin like a champ. That was some bold-ass shit. I mean, it was one thing to handle me like a hot pot with no handle, but to give me the note, like, "Here, old damn do-boy, go deliver this proclamation of disrespect," was truly foul.

They said experience was the best teacher and I learned a lot from my relationship with Kalia. Being sad wasn't even an option. I psyched myself out like nothing could hurt me.

Then I started thinking. Hold up. Was she hoping I read the note so she could break up with me? What gives? I had to save face though, so I went back to my Ice Cube mode while playing a "Bitch is a Bitch" in my mind. *Oh, it's like that? Cool. I'll play along like I hadn't read a thing.*

Even though I was getting played, in some warped sense, I felt like I had the upper hand. I remember watching Mya's face as she read the note in class. She looked up and glanced at me like, "You poor soul. You don't know what you're getting into."

No, I know. But two can play that game.

So, about a week or so after the note, I started to call Jasmine again and I began to call Dion a little less. Whenever we talked, Jasmine would drop little hints about Dion's shadiness. I figured this meant Jasmine knew about Dion's other boyfriend but just didn't have the heart to tell me. Was this why she had been acting different?

Still, I wasn't sure how this was gonna play out. *Wow, two times, back to back*, I thought, as we rode home from school one afternoon. Both girls cheated on me; is my game that weak? Maybe I wasn't exciting enough. Steve used to say girls like guys who were hard 'cause it made them feel alive to be around someone who did and said whatever. I was much too cautious, but I was me. I couldn't be someone else.

In a world full of self-respect and dignity I should have told Dion, "Hey, you're busted, and it's over."

However, something about having a girlfriend was almost like a trophy and I loved how it made me look and feel. So, at that time, even with what I knew, I swallowed it for the pride of having a girl. Was there a price to pay for my silence?

CHAPTER 21

IN LIVING COLOR

*"You can walk on the moon,
float like a balloon. You see you're
never too late and you're never too
soon. Take it from me, it's alright
to be...."*

-Heavy D

It was late April and a new comedy show called *In Living Color* had completely taken over television. The dancing girls in the intro were fly and I knew a lot of the actors from *Robert Townsend's Partners in Crime* specials on HBO. Reports of people dying from laughing were all over town and everyone at school imitated all the skits.

In my own personal skit that was my life, I didn't have a television audience, of course, but things were getting funnier by the day. Dion was playing me all the way out. Knowing this, I continued to kid around and flirt with Jasmine. Nothing serious, it was just two good friends being stupid. I even started writing her lil' notes and saying bogus stuff like, "Girl, you know I always loved you. Why are we playing games?" just to see what she would say.

One day, I poured out my feelings so strong in a note, that I think it confused her and she had to really wonder if I was for real. In truth, it was easy to say those things because I thought Jasmine was the shit. Not so much in a romantic way like a crush, it was more like a natural feeling from being so close to someone. She was my best friend and it felt so right, although I knew it was so wrong.

The day I gave Jasmine the fiery love note I wrote for her was interesting.

"Are you for real?" she asked. The look on her face told me she was thinking, *If you are, then I'm with it.*

Now, was she serious or playing a game like me? I could throw my cards on the table and say, "Well, I know you used to go with my best friend, but I don't care. I have to have you." Nah…she was my homie. Yet, the more I thought about it, the more I started to question if two people of the opposite sex could be good friends without being attracted to each other. I wasn't sure, but hooking up with Jasmine would have been the ultimate pay back for Dion.

But what about Malik? He had pretty much been my best friend since fifth grade. Trying to holler at Jasmine for real would have made me look foul and I value our friendship. So what do I do?

Maybe I'll break up with her after the eighth grade trip. No sense in being alone during a monumental moment of freedom in Orlando. And who knew what would happen? Maybe, somehow if I talked right, we would…

Yeah, the thoughts that ran through my head were riveting. I was becoming excited about the trip all over again. The ride, the pretty girls, the junk food, and most of all- no parents. I had been thinking about the trip all day when Malik ran up to me after our last class.

"Hey Dez," he started in a frenzy. "You seen that dude from Tatemville get jumped by Liberty City?"

"Nah, I missed it, who was brawlin'?"

He couldn't talk fast enough. "Your cousin, Marcus, Reg, that dude named Lo and some more boys from out there. They stomped that man into wine. Word is all them boys 'pose to fight again after school."

"Where at?" I looked around at the people coming up the hall.

"I don't know," Malik said.

"You gon' help your cousin and them?"

I took a long deep breath. "Nah, I really don't want to get in it. I'm not fin to let anyone jump my cousin, though."

"Damn, that's a tough spot to be in. If you don't help, them boys might look at you funny, bruh."

"Yep. If you see Marcus, tell him I'm looking for him."

"Hey, when you coming back? You been in Liberty City a minute."

"I'm not sure at all." I walked off looking in every direction. *Where was Marcus?*

As I boarded the Liberty City bus that afternoon, I felt the tension in the air. There was almost no one on the bus from Liberty City although Tatemville was deep as hell.

Yep, No Marcus and no Big Reg.

Right before we hit the first stop, folks from Tatemville started talking junk.

"Don't act scary now, Lo."

After they all laughed, my cousin's friend, Lo, stood up. "What y'all want to do? I ain't scared of nobody." He flexed his hands and took off his book bag.

Then someone from Tatemville snuck up from behind and boxed him in the mouth. It looked like he got hit with a hammer. He tried to fight back, but fell like a baby learning to walk. Then two boys kicked and stomped him a couple times until the bus driver slammed on the brakes. Everybody was yelling and throwing all kind of junk in the aisle and out the window. Lo looked up at me, but I didn't move.

"It ain't over," he kept yelling once he got up.

Then when we pulled up in Tatemville, he ran off the bus to fight the dudes who jumped him. Since he had lost the first round, I thought getting off was a big mistake. I mean *big mistake.*

He got off and was greeted by three dudes who jumped on every square inch of him at once. Then some other dudes from the neighborhood joined in so that made it about six to one. I noticed one of the dudes fighting him was the guy I hit with the volleyball back in gym class. People on the bus were in shock, and a lot of the girls were screaming for them to stop while the bus driver called for help.

"Shit, I'm about to go help this man," a guy named James yelled out as he looked at me. "You be out here in Liberty City. What's up?"

Just when I was deciding what to do, the guy I had beef with from gym class ran onto the bus to fight me.

"Nigga, I told you I was gon' get you," he popped off.

I had been boxing with my cousin and Big Reg and felt as ready as ever. He charged down the aisle and took a wild swing that missed and hit the seat. Then, I backed up and popped him twice in the face.

"Hellllll yeah," everybody, I mean everybody from Liberty City cheered. "Get that nigga ass."

Then we locked up and he threw me down into the seat. He hit me with a few shots in my stomach while I caught him again in the mouth. Finally, just as he tried to swing again, James came over and boxed him in the head.

Once he saw James was going to fight him too, he ran off the bus just as the cops pulled up. Lo got back on the bus after the beating he took and was fuming. He had damn near been crucified. I felt bad for him but all I could do was wonder where everybody else was. I felt my face to see if I had any bruises and I noticed Lo sweatin' me. *Was he mad that I didn't help him? Should I have? I didn't even know him like that.*

I got off the bus at the stop in Liberty City, and hauled ass to my cousin's house to see if he was there. When I made it to his street, my mom was unexpectedly pulling up in the driveway.

"Hey, what's going on? Why you running?" she asked.

"Uhhh, no reason. You were just here the other day, why you back so soon?"

She grabbed my chin and turned my face to the side. "Boy, what's wrong with your face?"

"Oh, we were playing football at school. I'm straight."

"Well you don't look straight, you ready to go home? We're leavin' in a few."

"Home?" I couldn't believe it.

"Yes, we're going home. You do have a home, don't you?" she teased.

Wow. No pre-planning. No warning. No nothing. Everything was put to a halt, just like that. So I went in to pack. About an hour passed and I had just finished packing before Marcus came in. He was mad and his shirt was torn around the collar.

"Dag, what happened to you?"

"I was just about to ask you the same thing," he said looking at my face.

I didn't have time to tell my cousin everything that happened, so I tried to talk quick. "Yeah, they beat Lo down."

He sat down on the bed. "And nobody helped him?"

"It wasn't anybody on the bus. I don't know bruh like that, but James, who stay by Reggie, was 'bout to help him and he motioned me to get up. I wasn't sure what I wanted to do, but then this dude in Tatemville I had beef with, got on the bus to fight me and we went at it."

"Damn Dez, for real?" he asked throwing a few punches at the air.

"Bruh, where were you and Reg?"

"We fought with some dudes from Tatemville 'cross the street from the school. Somebody swung on one of my partners and so we all got in it. Reg got arrested too. Man, it's gon' be hell on the bus tomorrow…" He shook his head.

"I don't know, the cops came in Tatemville, so some of them boys may not be in school."

He got up and took off his raggedy war-torn shirt.

"Man, I can't believe you leaving tonight."

"Yeah, I think things are straight at the house again, so this is it. I kinda don't want to go."

"Boy, you know you ready to go back to the 'Safe Southside'." He laughed.

"Man, shut up with that."

"Here." He handed me a box full of tapes that belonged to him. You'll get more out of these than me, I don't listen to half of this stuff."

"Man, I love this Redhead Kingpin album, thanks cuz."

"Hey, aren't you all going to Florida next week?" Marcus asked.

"Yep, for Spring Break."

He pulled out a condom to give me. "I heard y'all are going with a bunch of girls. Have fun, cuzo, but you still ain't getting none, punk," he joked.

"Whatever, what's the rubber for then?"

Just in case, some girl thinks your nerdy behind is halfway cool.

"Deeez," My mom yelled out for me. We dapped each other up and I headed downstairs. My aunt Shelia and mom were running their mouths about some of everything: Who got on their nerves this week at work and what happened around town.

Entering the living room, I interrupted them and gave my aunt a big hug. "Hey, Auntie Shelia, thanks for everything. I'm going to miss all of your good cooking.

"You're welcome, baby."

I couldn't exhale loud enough when I stepped outside. By this time, I was ready to hit the road, until I realized I forgot the rap I wrote to battle Tori. I went back inside and found it lying on the bed. I couldn't help but stare around the room I had slept in for the last month. In the last 40 days, it was like I lived another lifetime. Robberies, dope deals, pistol whippings, boxing matches, sneaking out, fights, and I almost lost my virginity to a crackhead. Yeah, I'd say it was a pretty wild month. Now I was headed home looking forward to the trip but watching my back for Tatemville.

CHAPTER 22

JACK THE RIPPER

"Back for the payback, I must say that,
I heard your new jam, I don't play that. It ain't loud
enough. Punk it ain't hittin'. This year you tired, next
year you quittin."

-LL Cool J

Late April 1990

When I walked inside my house, my mind flashed
back to the event that caused me to stay in Liberty City in
the first place. I could still see my stepdad running outside
in his draws; that was a crazy ass night. My mom said
they were getting along now but life for me had changed.
I peeked in my brother's room and noticed how empty it
was. It looked like he hadn't been there in weeks.

I walked into mama's room. "Where's Rich?"

She sighed. "Carolina, thank God."

"Carolina?"

"Yep, he went in the service. I rather he do that, than just sit round here."

My mom said he joined the Marines, but it didn't make sense. This was the same person who quoted "Black Steel in the Hour of Chaos" backwards and forwards; now he had given up his freedom to fight for something he didn't really believe in? Rich had done stuff in high school I couldn't even imagine doing: Stealing the car, hiding out with his girl in the attic, and lying about what school he went to when he got left back. So maybe he was looking for, as my stepdad said it, "*Discipline.*" Or he may have just wanted to move out and this was the best way to do it.

Yeah, it was going to be quieter around the house without ol' Rich. If he had been there, I would have talked to him about Liberty City and asked for his advice on a few things. Now I had to come up with some answers on my own.

I wish I could say I returned home to a rolled out red carpet and some horns, but the neighborhood was pretty much the same as I had left it. I saw everyone at school, so I only missed things that happened afterwards.

The next morning after I came back, I knocked on Shawn's door to throw his football around before the bus came.

When we all got on the bus, it was right back to the foolishness. "Brother, I'm glad you're back so you can keep the trees from growing. It wasn't the same without the neighborhood beaver," Khalil cracked.

I didn't have a quick rebuttal for him, but since Shawn laughed, I jumped on him instead. "How's that spelling going?"

He looked around to get everyone's attention. "I can still spell Kalia, though, fool."

"*Ooohhh,*" they all shouted welcoming me back.

To be funny, Malik touched me with one finger like I was burning hot.

"Yeah, I know that one stung."

"Don't let Shawn talk junk. Girls stay dumping him. They just be ugly, so we don't hear about it," Steve said while standing up to put on his Walkman.

It was a familiar scene, and that morning we all went back and forth until everybody was out of jokes. This meant that things were indeed back to normal.

Later that day after school, I noticed how much the dye in my hair had faded since Atlanta. Luckily, I had found my old trusty bottle of Sun In and I was ready to experiment. I wanted to get my hair fresh again for the big trip to Orlando. I was 'bout ready to start when Malik called and said he was coming over. When he knocked on the door, I was in the bathroom finishing up.

"What the hell is Sun In?"

"Something I used on me, Head and Shawn to dye our hair."

He put his nose next to the bottle to smell it. "Man, them boys let you put that jive in their head?"

"Fasho." I snatched the bottle and sprayed on some more.

"Yeah, y'all are even dumber than I thought."

"Why you say that? You just scared to get fresh." I bumped him out of the way.

He pointed to my hair and smirked. "Nah, my dad been pulled me to the side and said, 'Look at that shit on ya friends' heads. They following up with what everyone else doing—learn to be yourself.'"

"So what you really saying is you like the dye, but your dad won't let you have fun, huh?" I cracked.

"Man, I ain't studdin' you; you understand what I'm sayin.'"

I had no idea what I was doing then or before, but once the sun hit my hair, it actually didn't look half bad.

I was going on and on about Liberty City the whole time Malik was at my house. We had been in my room playing video games for hours until Steve called.

"Dez, quick. I need you to come over. I gotta show you something."

"What you got, bruh?"

"Man, come on., I don't have time to explain."

When I told Malik what Steve said, he laughed. "Show you something? Now, I know you know: that man up to something dumb."

I didn't have a clue what it was, but after we finished our game we went to see what was up. When we arrived, everybody in the surrounding neighborhoods were outside playing basketball at Steve's.

"There go Dez," a couple guys hollered.

I thought they were ready to play a game, so I ran up and snatched a ball from Steve to shoot it. I took a shot and just as I hit the rim, Tori, the guy who battled me in rapping at the beginning of the school year, came bopping around the corner.

Tori had got into a program to get back in his right grade, so he had been going to high school for quite a while. When he came around the corner, everybody except for me already knew what time it was. We were due for another battle and Steve and a few other people had set it up.

So this was the surprise—a setup, I said to myself.

FLICTED

Looking my way, Malik nonchalantly raised his eyebrows.

Everybody began to crowd around.

"What's up? That man Dez said he fresher than you now, Tori," Steve goaded.

"Well, I did mention to Steve that I wanted to battle Tori's wack ass while I was in Liberty City," I whispered to Malik.

Malik looked at me and shook his head. "Well, you better prove it."

Tori said something to Steve when he walked up and then he turned toward me with a real sinister look. "So what up, nigga?"

"What up, nigga?" I retorted.

Then Tori got ready to set it off. "All right, you know what it is. Who got a beat?"

Though Fat didn't care for Tori, he immediately came in with something and the mood was set. Tori bopped his head a couple times before he started, like he was rehearsing in his mind, then he came out firing. His rhymes had pit bull bite, and I knew he didn't like me.

"That mama boy shit is done when I come
Point me to that nigga that said he want some
DDT, suplex, I'll pile drive 'em
get in touch quick with that girl inside him
raid heart staying pumping Kool-Aid
Black Freddy Krueger; keep suckers afraid
Never be shit when you don't got guts
you a squirrel type of nigga come and hold my
nuts."

215

"Ohhh my God," the crowd jeered.

Fat paused and looked at me as if to say, "You sure you want to go through with it?" But there was no fear.

"My bad, Dez, I ain't know he was gon' do you like that," Steve gasped, but he knew...

This time, I was ready to throw shots back.

> *"Why o' Why, do you want to flauge?*
> *From the Southside yellin' Westside hard*
> *I'ma be me, nigga, nobody else*
> *Want it? Come get it. I'm bad for ya health*
> *Last time, you caught me off guard*
> *Now you on ya' knees calling out to GOD*
> *Hands up.... I put this between ya eyes*
> *You stank like ya mama don't wash between*
> *her thighs."*

Yeah, it got ugly quick. After round one, he hit me with some lines about my mama, my girlfriend, what I had on, and everything else you could think of. I returned the favor, talked about his mom, plus how he had gotten beat up. We went at it wild and reckless until we both started to stumble through our last raps.

The crowd kept spicing it up and it felt like we were about to fight for real, but it stayed confined to a tongue submission.

He had more raps memorized, but he was not ready for the way I could freestyle and make up things on the spot. I kept pulling in stuff from around us to rap about and it made people take notice.

After the battle, he still tried to talk a lil' junk, but came over and dapped me anyway.

"I can't front; you got a lot better, bruh."

I nodded with a firm facial expression. "Word, you still be busting too."

"We gon' battle again, though." he said walking off with some other dudes who had just lit up a joint to smoke. Once my adrenaline stopped pumping, I walked over to my crew. "Well, what y'all think? Who won?"

Malik looked indecisive for a second. "You had some real fresh lines, I think you got him. You're starting to get your own voice, too. It doesn't sound so much like other people now."

Fat dapped me up. "R-E-S-P-E-C-T."

"Thanks, bruh."

"Y'all were alright, but y'all better not battle me," Shawn said, being silly.

I stood next to him to be somewhat intimidating. "Well, where your raps at, Don King, since you were hyping it up?"

"I got some, don't worry, I'm working. I can't let you be only person representin' for our hood," Shawn joked.

"Hey, Shawn, you ready for the trip to Orlando." I asked.

"Am I? I got me a new girl, too, and she going-going, 'cause I'm flowin-flowin. You like that, right? I'ma get it all night."

"Hey." Steve walked up. "Man, don't be mad at me. I wanted you to battle him and prove you were the best."

Malik's face looked like he knew Steve was lying. "You sure you didn't want him to lose?"

"Nah, for real." He put both if his hands in the air like he was being arrested, then smirked. "Look, I'll make it up to you. I got this freak coming through."

I squinted my face at him. "Who?"

"That lil' redbone from over there on Middleground Road."

Steve looked at Shawn. "You still down, right?"

Shawn nodded.

I couldn't believe it. "So, both of y'all are about to have sex with her?"

Steve gyrated his waist. "Yeah, we 'bout to run a train."

"A train?" Fat asked, confused.

"I'm telling you, we can all get some." Steve pumped his fist into his hand. "She said to come get her around six and it was cool to bring whoever. My mama don't get home til eight. That's gives us about two hours of action."

Malik looked at Shawn real funny. "Bruh, you gon' follow up with Steve, huh?"

Steve bumped my shoulder before hopping on his bike. "Dez, you down? I'm about to go get her little freaky ass."

"Man, isn't she in the sixth grade?" I questioned, but after the trip to the crackhead's house, I was in no position to play holier than thou.

Fat backed up from us. "Y'all negroes going to jail."

"Jail? She ain't but two years younger than us. Nobody making her do anything. If she didn't want it, she wouldn't be coming," Shawn declared.

Malik just looked at Shawn and shook his head. "What, you want me to walk around with blue balls like Fat?" Shawn joked.

"First of all," Fat began, looking mad as hell. 'What man is concerned 'bout another man's penis anyway? Look here: when I do get some, it won't be like y'all. Why the heck would I wanna run up in something after y'all trifling Negroes put your jive in it? Nah, I'm straight."

"Fat is delusional. Some girls are like that, and they like that kind of stuff," Shawn said, like some sort of expert.

Fat responded, "Okay, maybe, but if they do, you ever asked yourself why?"

In his best comedic tone, Shawn announced, "'Cause they just like it. They like that ding-a-ling-a-ling, so they can sing-a-sing, sing."

Finally, Fat said, "Yeah, talking with you is a waste of time." He threw up a peace sign and walked off.

Not too long after that, Steve came around the corner with the girl. She smiled, then rubbed Shawn on his shoulder after speaking to everyone. Steve told her to hold up and then he came over to us.

"What's up? This y'all last chance." Steve looked at her, then back at us. "Y'all some lames, you don't see all that boonkie in them jeans?"

"I'll be lame then," Malik blew him off. "C'mon man, we ain't got nothin' to do with that. Let's walk to the store."

Sex made us all take huge risks and this was one I'm glad I didn't take. On the way to the store, I ended up talking to Malik about Dion a little—nothing too heavy. I was damn sure too embarrassed to talk about the note and I knew I couldn't mention the stuff about Jasmine. But maybe I should have. I mean, if we were like brothers, I should be able to tell him anything...right?

The big trip was a day away, so I packed my bags and thought about the fun I was going to have. How many times would I get a chance to take a trip like this out of town with a bunch of friends and my girl? Carefully, I put a plan together on how to handle Dion. Now, I just had to put it all in place. Nobody plays D-E-Z and gets away with it.

CHAPTER 23

I DO NEED YOU

"But if I keep holding on,
Just maybe you'll see
That I do need you, I want you."

-BBD

Early May 1990

The day of the trip, I was pure electricity. I leaped out from under the covers to take my rightful place in the rich history of crazy adolescence. Every young person deserves an unforgettable class trip and this morning was the start of mine. I ended up on the bus with Shawn, his new girlfriend, and a ton of cool folks that I knew from around school. Dion, Briana, Mya, and a lot of other girls were on the second bus.

I won't front, I got excited when I saw Dion. She had on a pair of sweatpants with a funky hat turned to the back and she looked cuter than ever. My headphones were pumping loud and I was chilling, waiting on the bus to pull off for the trip.

Shawn sat down beside me and pointed out the window. "I see ya girl and them on the other bus."

I tried to act like it didn't matter. "Yeah, I saw her."

Leaning back in the seat, I figured it would give Dion and I a chance to miss each other, so I joked with Shawn until I heard this familiar giggle. I used to love that laugh; now, I hated it.

Kalia came stepping up on the bus looking all good with her new boyfriend. Yep, she strutted down the aisle with the white guy from the dance like they were a new and improved version of us. Guess, I wasn't light enough, huh?

Shawn's girlfriend insisted that the white dude and Kalia were just friends and that she liked talking with him because he was different.

"Different?" I asked thinking about our relationship.

"Yeah, she says he pays attention and is really into what she has to say."

Man, that's bull, she doesn't even talk that much, or was she just quiet with me?

Just beneath the surface, rumors were floating around about who was supposed to be hooking up at the hotel. Shawn was cuddled up with his new girl and I started to think about Dion. *What is this girl up to? Why play with me? Is this my big chance to get off the Virgin Islands? Should I teach her a lesson?*

While I was going through question after question in my mind, Shawn turned around and tapped me on the shoulder. "Hey, Dez, switch tapes with me. I want to listen to that new Ice Cube you were playing earlier. What's it called?"

"AmeriKKKa's Most Wanted. What tape you got?"

"I got that new BBD; you heard it?"

"Nah, but we can switch."

Every song on BBD's album was bangin' and I jammed it all the way 'til we pulled in at a rest stop. Once we got off the bus to stretch, I went to find Dion.

"Hey Dez, did you miss me?" She put her hand over her heart and threw her head back.

Playing along I started acting goofy and hugged her like I had found my long lost love at the end of a corny movie.

Everybody looking at us was laughing.

"You are soo special, stop being silly, Dez." She cracked up.

Then, she grabbed my hand and twirled herself around.

"Oh, let's take some pictures. Mya has her camera."

Everything felt fun and free like young love.

Dion started looking better and better; yet, I knew I couldn't let myself really fall for her after that note. It was all just a game, right?

When we arrived in Orlando, we stopped in the heart of downtown to get a quick bite to eat, before we made our way to the hotel. Our rooms were kind of fancy, but of course, everyone was more concerned about girls. It was about ten of us piled up in a room checking and rating girls for the evening events. We made so much noise people probably heard us down the street. But there was no way to control all that testosterone.

Finally, we all changed our clothes and washed up to get ready for dinner. I was ready to eat and excited to be excited, if that makes sense. As men, we took the offense and walked down to the hotel floor where a lot of girls were staying, hoping they would hear us and come out.

We walked past their rooms, tapped on a few doors, and yelled out some obscene jokes. Then, like magic, they appeared.

"Dez, your girl wants to see you," Mya announced to the whole hallway.

Everybody all at once was like, "*Whaaat.*"

Too pumped up to think, I went into the room with no real expectations other than a hug. Dion had given me a peck or two in the past, but it wasn't anything worth writing about. However, this was different. The room was dimly lit with one lamp. She had on a pair of tight jeans and tank top. Her bra was on top of the bed.

"Derrick, come here," she said, real sultry-like.

"What's up?"

I walked across her hotel room and froze for a sec. We were standing right in front of the lamp and I could see through her top. Then, she grabbed me. Looking deep into my eyes, she held the back of my neck and slowly pulled me toward her. For me, a homerun would have been a tight embrace of lips. Instead, she threw her tongue *way down* my throat.

I had no clue, and when I say no clue, I mean *none*. If you had asked before that moment, I would have said French kissing was for… the French. I mean, I saw it in the movies, but I didn't know black people kissed like that. I was that clueless. I slobbered and drooled on her quite a bit when we kissed, but it felt great nonetheless. Her warm mouth and tongue were the sweetest things I had ever known.

She smiled and squeezed my back while putting her tongue in my mouth again. It was squishy and delicious and I wanted more. Before I knew it, we were up against the wall rubbing on each other.

She was breathing heavy. "Hey Dez, we gotta stop."

"Huh, what?" I managed to say with my little friend bulging by my zipper.

"We gotta stop, everyone's heading down for dinner."

"Oh yeah, dinner. Can we... hook up later?"

"Well, we'll see, won't we?" She laughed when I wiped the drool from the side of my mouth.

I was embarrassed. "Damn, my bad."

"It's alright. Now I have something else to clown you about."

Afterwards, we went down for dinner, but I couldn't get her off my mind. I kept seeing us kissing over and over...and over...the entire evening. I had totally forgotten about the note.

I've got to get to her room, to get some more of that...

That night, the guys in my room thought about all kinds of ways to escape. We wanted girls so bad, scaling the walls outside weren't out of the question, until, our chaperones caught wind. By the time they rounded everyone up, we had heard of stories of people getting it on. Most were probably exaggerations but a few were hot, steamy, and very much true. Mr. Jenks came to check on us around midnight, and emphasized that at this point, we better stay in our room or else.

It was late, but with Dion on my mind, I was far from tired. I threw on BBD in my headphones and played all of the slow jams to pass the time. When I made it to "I Do Need You," that song, along with the kiss she put on me, had me rethinking my life. Figuring Shawn wasn't asleep, I yanked the covers off his head. "Hey, how you made out with your girl?"

"Boy, she smelled so good. That baby powder and that perfume she had on was workin."

"Hey, bruh, guess what? Dion straight threw her tongue down my throat. I mean way down."

"Was she a good kisser?" he asked.

"Of course," I said, as if I had something to compare her to. I couldn't say she was my first real kiss, so....

"Okay, so what else did you do?"

"What do you mean, what else...I mean we kind of grinded on each other a little bit."

He got out the bed and sat down next to me. "Man, me and my girl got busy. All you did was kiss. You act like it was your first time...I thought you told Steve you wasn't no virgin."

"Nah... but it was other people in her room. I couldn't do anything."

"I get it, but you were so hyped, I just thought you may have gotten some."

"Like you and Steve the other day?"

"Man, I didn't even do anything with that freak. Steve stayed in his room with her so long, I just left."

He hopped back in his bed. "Hey, you getting real cozy with that BBD tape. I'ma need it back 'fore you start hunching on it."

"You silly, bruh, let me jam." And with that, I turned up the volume and floated away to think about Dion all night.

For the rest of the trip, every chance I got, I was holding her hand with the utmost pride. It was almost like she had some sort of bell, and when she rang, I quickly appeared with my tux and white gloves. I had fallen in love with Dion even when I knew better.

Mid May 1990

Once we got back from the trip, we talked on the phone way more than before.

"Dez, I'm coming to see you," she told me on the phone. "I'll be at Mya's house this Thursday after school. Where can I meet you at?"

I began to breathe hard. "Can you meet me at Malik's?" This would let everyone know I was the man.

That day, they walked up while we were playing ball. I was so proud to see her that I grabbed her by the hand in front of all my friends to show her off. Then, when I got the chance, I took her on the side of Malik's house. In broad daylight, we exchanged tongues and expressed our love. It felt so good. I could barely hear Mya trying to break us up.

"Hey, girl, we gotta go. Your mama will be there at six to pick you up."

It was about 5:30. So to save time, they hopped the fence in Malik's backyard to head back to her neighborhood. That night when she called to let me know she made it home safely I totally bugged out.

"Girl, I just wanna snatch your clothes off and do some things. I'm on fire 'round here; if I don't do something soon, somebody gon' have to throw a bucket of ice water on me."

"So are you saying you love me?" she asked.

"Yes, and I do need you," I pleaded pathetically.

During this time, she even became the object of my raps and that was sacred territory. I was spending quality time putting lyrics together about her, and then I built up the courage to leave a rap called "I Think You Fly" on her answering machine. I wrote it to LL Cool J's, "I Need Love."

> *D is for delightful.*
> *I intelligent*
> *Outstanding, and*
> *Nice*
> *it's like you heaven-sent,*
> *you can smile all day with your beautiful eyes.*
> *When we talk, at night, the more I realize*
> *You're special, to me in a unique way*
> *So I wrote this jam.*
> *Got something to say*
> *In L-O-V...E, where I want to be*
> *In ya arms, you and me, feelin' so damn free.*
> *Hey Dion, tell me how can you respond*
> *love to kiss on your body 'til the break of dawn.*
> *Why...?*
> *I could be with you til' I die*
> *yeah my heart beats forever*
> *and I Think You Fly..."*

"Ahh, Dez, that was sooo cute—I love it and you. You know I'm 'bout to save this on my machine forever, right?" So, finally—*no, seriously, finally*—I had to be with her.

The next day after school, I walked to our bus to find Malik.

"Look, if my mom asks you where I'm at, tell her I stayed after school with Mr. Jenks."

"Okay, what you up to?" he asked.

"I'm going to see Dion, bruh."

"Woah…you going to her house? I hear you pimp."
Then he looked at me square in the eyes. "Be careful,
though."

When I got there, something hit me and I paused a
sec. *What if her parents are home? Okay, I'ma ask if Reg
is there and make like I had the wrong house.*

I mustered up all my confidence, pimped across the
street and knocked on the door. She was always home by
herself when we talked on the phone after school, so I just
knew the situation would be perfect.

I had every intention of getting busy even though we
hadn't talked about anything directly. It was implied. I
told her I was on fire, check. She kissed me at the hotel,
check. I done walked all 'round her house, double check.
Time to get busy. Ha, I still didn't have a condom, even if
I did I wouldn't know what to do with it. Last time I
opened a condom, I was in fourth or fifth grade.

"Why is this balloon so greasy?" I had asked. I gave
the one Marcus had given me to Shawn.

Anyway, I knocked and knocked like the Big Bad
Wolf, but no one came to the door. She was always home.
What gives? I didn't know what to think. I was tired and I
started to feel foolish about it all. Then it came to me:
even though she wasn't there, I somehow had to prove I
came. *Yes, she needed to know my level of commitment.*
So, I bought a black spray can from the store and painted
our initials inside of a heart, on an electric pole by her
house.

Ramo from *Beat Street* gave me that stupid idea. I
had lost it. I was officially cuckoo for Cocoa Puffs for this
girl that I now, had to have.

FLICTED

Heading home, I caught the bus from Liberty City to downtown and walked around until my transfer. Then, I heard someone call out my name. I turned around and it was my stepdad's sister. I didn't think about the fact that I shouldn't actually be downtown, so I spoke to her like everything was cool.

"Hey, Auntie."

She wore a concerned look on her face. "What are you doing downtown?"

"Oh, I'm just coming from school," I said, like it was no big deal to be downtown by myself.

"Oh, okay. Good to see you, baby. Tell your mom I said hi."

After she left, my first thought was, "Dag, that went well." Almost too well.

I know this bus need to hurry up, I thought. I passed the time watching this funny old dude asking everybody for change. He looked drunk and at first, I thought he was talking out the side of his neck.

"Y'all don't see our people laying over there in Whitfield Square? They asking me if the city haunted. You don't hear 'em?" he asked.

"Huh, hear who?" another guy at the bus stop said out loud.

"You better listen. Hey, you ain't got no change for me? You know I marched with King, who you marched with? You got something to march for?" he asked me.

"Man, I had a rough day. All I got is thirty five cents...."

"Boy, I woke up with the HAG this morning. I wasn't sure I was gonna make it, but here I am and you look worse than me. You wanna hold something?" He laughed.

231

I didn't know if he was for real or not, but it did take my mind off Dion for a sec. I wanted to give up but after coming this far, nothing was going to stop me from sexing her.

CHAPTER 24

HEY YOUNG WORLD

*"Have you forgotten who
put you on this earth,
who raised you up right
who loved you since birth."*

-Slick Rick

With sex so close, I knew I was becoming a man. My walk, my style, and my attitude were changing by the day. I had just come in from Malik's when my brother, Paul, and Nia stopped by for a visit. After they came in and talked awhile, my brother took my mom to handle something while Nia stayed behind.

"How were things in Liberty City?" she asked.

"Crazy. I had fun out there, but sometimes it was wild as hell. What about you?"

"Look Derrick, I was in class the other day and I heard this dude say some boys in Tatemville were supposed to be jumping you because you helped Liberty City fight against them. And then this other dude in our class said Lo wanted to fight you for not helping him, but he couldn't because of Marcus."

At first I was stuck. "Help? I wasn't about to help nobody. I was just defending myself." I cracked my knuckles. "Well, whatever, I ain't worried 'bout them or Lo's sorry ass."

I tried to play it down, but I was scared and the way she looked made it worst. Now, I didn't know why I did it, but I left the room and came back with something to kill all the talk.

"Look, if they jump me, they're in for a surprise."

Then, I showed her the .357 Magnum that belonged to my stepdad as if it were mine. I pointed it toward the ceiling, then, I laid it beside her so she would know that it was real.

I had never come close to picking up his gun before, but in that moment, I felt compelled to show her I wasn't playin'. She looked at me, aiming that gun around the room, and her eyes lit up like a Christmas tree. She didn't know what to say until I pointed the gun at myself in the mirror.

"Are you crazy? What are you doing with a gun?" she screamed.

The way she looked was how I wanted everyone else to look; terrified. The cops, the guy who pistol whipped Reg, and all them fools in Tatemville. I was foolishly entering the same cycle of violence without even realizing it.

Damn, what was I doing? I'm not about to shoot no one. Then the front door opened.

"Dez quick, you better put that gun up," Nia said full of nerves.

There was no time to, so I opened my window and sat it outside 'til I could figure out when to put it back. Later, while my mom was at the door telling my brother good bye, I snuck and placed it back from where I'd had taken it. Then, I pretended like it never happened.

A day or so later, when I walked in, my mom cracked open the ceiling from calling my name.

"Derriiick?"

"Well, here goes the one millionth and first time," I said, not knowing what was coming.

Yet this time, there was more fire on the end of that K than usual. Something must be...up.

"Why were you downtown the other day and where the hell did you get a gun from?"

"A gun?" I repeated.

"Yes, you heard me. I said *gun*. Nia told your brother that she was worried about you 'cause some boys were 'posed to be fightin' you and you showed her a gun."

I usually kept at least one undetectable lie in my head to get out of a bad situation, but I was speechless. I felt these sharp pains running all through my body like I was about to collapse.

"Where did I get a gun from?" I asked her again, trying to buy some time to think.

I mean, I could have come clean and said that it was my stepdad's gun. Nah, that would have made too much sense. So I paused. "Uhhh... Marcus."

"*Marcus,*" she yelled, and then proceeded to scream at me for another five minutes. It seemed like at any moment she was going to lose it and skin me alive down to the bone.

"I'm going to call my sister right now." She stormed out of the room.

Uh oh, this won't be good.

If I could have, I would have given Marcus a heads-up. I knew before it was over that I was going to get my ass cut. To be honest, I got scared. I almost believed that I really did get the gun from him. Standing in the hallway, I could hear my mom and his mom talking on the phone, and his mom was steaming. Next thing ya' know, my mom had her keys in her hand and said, "We're going to their house *right now.*"

Again, I had every opportunity to come clean; I just couldn't. I let my mom drive all the way across town to Liberty City, walk into my cousin's house and basically look stupid.

"Girl, I don't know what's going on. Marcus swears he didn't give Derrick no gun."

My mom took a deep breath while listening to my aunt talk and after she watched my mom collect herself, my aunt continued, "Usually I know he'll lie sometimes, but his dad was in there beating him to death and I could tell he was telling the truth."

My cousin came downstairs looking like he had been through hell with his dad. When he saw me, he looked at me, then looked away like, "Nigga, you for real?"

I knew he had lost a lot of respect for me, and by the look in his eyes, there was no way to get it back any time soon.

"Stop lying right now and tell me where you got the gun," my mom yelled again.

The interrogation was intense and I knew I wasn't going to make it. Under pressure, I did what I should have done three hours and three dollars' worth of gas ago. I told her the gun belonged to my stepdad.

Well, that wasn't so bad and I felt relieved to get it off my chest—until she told me to take off my belt.

"Pull your pants down." There was no white in her eyes. All I saw was blackness.

"But Ma..."

Before I could get another syllable out... "Whap!" The belt slashed across the back of my head, buckle and all on its way to landing on my butt. I got beat not only for the gun, but for everything else I had gotten away with that year.

My mom was beside herself with anger. "You lied to me. I can't believe I defended you. I wanted to believe Marcus made you do it." She stopped to get her second wind. "It was you all along." Whap! Whap!

"Mama...? Listen...!" I screamed.

"I don't know who you think you are talking to in that tone, boy."

Something that had been so insignificant to me at the time had come back to bite me hard.

I was on serious lockdown for about three weeks and my mom didn't talk to me at all. I hadn't been allowed to do anything but breathe until my brother, Melvin came to check on me. I was in my room counting the paint specks on the ceiling.

"Hey grab your shoes, let's go hoop." He threw the ball to me.

I looked at him strange. "I don't know if Mama's going to let me."

"Nah, I talked to her."

When we made it to the court, he gave me a look like my dad would give me, and I knew he was disappointed. "Lil' bruh, what's going on?"

At first I didn't say anything, then after I missed a couple of shots I started, "Well, I know you heard how bad I messed up."

He shook his head. "Yeah, I'm trying to figure that out."

"Man, I don't even know, it was just dumb... I wasn't thinking."

"I was surprised. I thought maybe you had a BB gun, but then Mama said you got the gun out of their room." He backed me down in the hole for a shot.

"Please don't remind me. I get sick every time I think about the ass whooping I got."

"I bet you did, that was serious." He shot me quick elbow in the chest to make space for his shot. "Look, I'ma say this, you have to make better choices. That could have cost you or Nia your lives."

I was so nervous that I couldn't dribble without losing the ball. "Yeah, she screamed when I showed it to her. I just want the whole incident to go away but it won't."

"Yep, that's called your conscience, the voice of God within us. It's there to remind you to do the right thing."

I swiped at the ball in his hands, but he was too quick. "I wished it had reminded me before I did it," I said.

"It may have, the question is, were you listening? Lil bruh, I love you. Everyone makes mistakes, but the mark of real man is what you do afterwards. This is AFTERWARDS. If you having any problems, call me, I'm always here."

Melvin's talk was supportive even though I had messed up. However, the rest of my family was not and everyone had something to say.

"He's smart and all, but watch: he is going to end up in jail," I heard Paul tell my mom. "Next thing you know, he'll be stealing and selling drugs."

With omens like that, you'd think I would have followed my mom's rules from then on out, but temptation is hard to resist. Dion saw me in the hall and said she was going to the mall with Mya after school. I calculated the time and figured I could stop and see her, then make it home before my mom.

That afternoon we were standing in the mall by the Tilt Arcade talking and holding hands, when Dion and Mya suddenly went crazy.

"Marvin, Marvin, it's Marvin." they cried out.

Marvin was a dude I hadn't seen since the seventh grade. We used to play on a little league basketball team together until he moved to Virginia or somewhere up North.

"Ooh, Marvin, we miss you. Are you moving back to Savannah?" Dion asked.

He cocked his head back and gloated, "I just came for the week to visit my dad, but I'm moving back this summer."

I was super jealous. I thought, *If it's like that when you go away and come back, maybe Alabama ain't so bad after all."*

I made it back before my mom that evening just like I had planned, then I called my dad. It was official. I told him I would move to Alabama for next school year.

Meanwhile, I was still living on the Virgin Isles and very much on punishment and very much thinking about my immediate future. Would my mom let me go? Would Dion finally give me some, once I told her that I was leaving? After all this work, she has to.

CHAPTER 25

DOWHATCHALIKE

"Homegirls, for once,
forget you got class.
See a guy you like:
just grab him in the biscuits."

-Digital Underground

Late May 1990

Yes. Something that could take me away from all the trouble I was in at home...*yearbooks*. Yearbooks were a treasure in middle school. So when you signed someone's, you wanted to make it count. Yearbooks were filled with many warm memories, but there was nothing like somebody showing out and dropping a bomb on one of your pages.

Girls specialized in this, and our year reviews were no different. There were crazy pictures and memories in them that would forever capture this moment in time. I couldn't wait to see what everyone had to say.

FLICTED

"'Keep in touch', 'Love you like a brother', 'Keep pimpin', yada ya."

On another note, yearbooks also meant I had to tough it out with my disappointing yearbook photo. My jives were always the worst. I was so self-conscious of my overbite that I never learned how to naturally smile. I always ended up lookin' like I swallowed a fish that was trying to jump out my mouth. Add that to the fact that I tried to look cool and *wallah*...you had one flicted-lookin' picture.

One of the first to sign my book was Briana:

"Dez, you are someone I started to get close with and it's been a trip. Hope there are great things in your future and I enjoyed all the little 'chit chats' that we had. It's nice that you are with Dion, but if things don't work out with her, I hope you find someone who fits your personality and knowledge level. I know you have bright future ahead of you so, stay out of trouble... Peace."

This made me smile, but I kinda wondered why she would even say, "if" things don't work out. *Did she know something I didn't?*

Kalia and I were speaking to each other again and when she asked to sign my yearbook, I felt honored. I mean, after all, it *was* Kalia.

"Dez, it was more than a pleasure knowing and being with you. I know I wasn't all you thought I was going to be, but I wish I could have been, maybe things would have been different if we would have been friends first. I wish we could do the year all over again. Remember me always, Kalia."

That made me feel good especially after all the tears I shed over her.

When I saw Jasmine in the hall, she shouted for the whole school to hear, "Dez, give me your yearbook next period. Save me a whole page."

She wrote the whole thing in big, bold, bright colors for all to see.

"Dez, it's been great knowing you. We really didn't get to know each other until I started going with Malik. It could have been you and I, but you wanted to act stuck up. I'm so glad we turned out to be best friends, but who knows? We might be able to hook up in the future. If we do, the future will bring you a good thing. I know Dion is going to be pissed when she reads this, but I don't care. I'll only live once and I'm expressing myself. She said she can't trust me and this should make her doubt me even more. I thought she was my friend but I was so wrong. Have a great summer and I know you'll be spending a lot of time with me. Love you lots, Jasmine.

I had no idea if she was for real, or not. Was she, and what was Dion gonna say when she saw her page in my book?

Well, it wasn't long 'fore I found out.

"Dear Dez, Right now and for the past couple of days, I have been jealous of Jasmine. You all are so close. I see everyone looks out for you when you get in a relationship. I had to tell Jasmine I couldn't trust her because why should I lie? I'm glad you put up with me, because we're still going strong. You had a lot of choices, but you picked me."

In the end, she signed my yearbook and gave me a picture of her that said, "I love you and I want you to come back to my house." She was ready and I was ready. Everything was perfect.

CHAPTER 26

JUST A FRIEND

"You, you got what I need
But you say he's just a friend
But you say he's just a friend."

-Biz Markie

Early June 1990

Finally, I was officially let out the dungeon my mom had kept me in. Other than the warning about her willingness to kill me and go to jail if I kept messing up, she didn't say much. That Saturday afternoon, I enjoyed my first taste of freedom with Steve at the mall. For the past few weeks he had been bragging about how many times he had sex with the girl who lived on Middleground.

"You not worried about getting caught?" I asked.

He stuck his chest out. "By who?"

"Her mom, your mom." I shrugged my shoulders.

"Nah…my mama knows I be having sex and I don't care about her mom," he smirked.

"'Sup with you and your girl? You hit that yet?"

I anxiously rubbed my hands together. "I'm 'bout to; she wants me to come over this week."

We had just walked from one side of the mall to the other, when Steve's eyes shot open. "Hold up bruh, isn't that your girl right there?"

I wiped my eyes like something was in them. "She damn sure ain't say she'd be here today."

But, there she was standing in the center of the mall talking to this football playing-looking joker. The whole scene just looked wrong, yet, instead of trying to deny anything, she called out, "Oh, hey Derrick, come here. There's someone I want you to meet."

So is he just a friend? I considered before opening my mouth to speak.

She put her arm around him and gave me the fakest smile ever. "Cedric, this is my boyfriend, Dez."

"What up?" he said, brimming with confidence and unwavering authority.

My gut feeling was, *Yep, you've been played* and in an instant, everything about that note from months ago came back to the forefront of my memory. Cedric was the name from the note Dion wrote to Mya. He was the fine ass boyfriend she couldn't give up.

I was pissed, especially when this dude looked at me. His smirk seemed to say, "Man, I be bustin' your girl down; shiiit, somebody has to do it."

As soon as she introduced him, I walked off. I wasn't about to play myself and fight over a girl. Plus, that joker looked bigger than three of me. *Long as he doesn't touch me,* I said to myself, while trying to keep my dignity.

Steve ran up quick. "Yo, why he all up on your girl? He looks like he's knockin' her boots or something, what's up? You wanna fight him?"

"Nah chill man, my beef is with her. I'll call her later and see what the deal is."

When I got home and thought about it, I wanted to believe that she could not be that foul. Had she still been going with him despite the Florida trip and all those kisses? *She had just told me to come back over.*

She seemed like a whole different person when I called that night. Or maybe this was who she was all along.

"Hey, what's up with you?" I asked ready to go off about the mall.

I heard a bunch of shuffling, then she put the phone on speaker to make sure I could hear. She began talking extremely loud to her sister.

"This nigga, Dez, though..."

"What up, Dion? What's the problem?" her sister asked, sounding like she was reading from a script.

"Man, I don't know what to do. I mean, he saw me with the other nigga in the mall and everything. His slow ass...this nigga is still calling me." She sounded very bothered. "I don't get it. Can a girl take the trash out or what?"

Slow? Trash?

That was all the abuse I could stomach. I hung up and never talked to her again.

My heart wasn't broken like Kalia had broken it, but the anger of being called "trash" and "slow" stung. It was as if my draws came down in the lunchroom and everyone at school was pointing at me standing with a limp one. I was naked with nowhere to hide. Was this what I deserved...had I reaped what I had sown? Furious, I started to hear the craziest things in my head:

"Hey, you a fool. We all knew."

"I tried to tell you. You were just her lil' middle school boo thang; that girl got a High School Man."

In my nightmare of a daydream, even the custodian poked his head out and said, "Yeah, bruh, I knew, too. Your slow ass."

"So, tell us, please, how does it feel to be absolutely made a fool of?"

"What, you thought you had game? You? Game? *Haaa.*"

And then with a stadium full of laughter, I knew it would be hard to hold my head high and trust a girl with my heart.

I was flicted.

During the last week of school, I bumped into Jasmine. We hadn't talked for about a week or so.

"Deeeez," she yelled down the hall. "So, are you really leaving?"

First, I smiled, then it turned into a fake frown. "Yeah, but I'm not sure if I'm going right after school's out or what. Will you miss me?" I asked.

She lightly slapped me on my head. "Of course, boy, you know you my best friend."

I gave her a hug from the side. "I gotta show you all the pictures I took. I have a nice one of you on Career Day; you looked so pretty in your business suit."

She kissed me with a quick peck on the cheek. "Ahh, thank you, come by my house and let me see all the pictures."

Okay...hold up, did she just kiss me.

I had another *what if* moment. I hadn't taken what she wrote in my yearbook serious. *Should I have? Was this just a friendly, hey homie, kiss or was I being slow yet again?*

Without a second thought, I decided I was going to walk to her house, look her in the face with those sexy lips she had and say, "What's up?" If she was for real, I planned to go for it on the spot. Boldness. That's what I needed.

At the end of the day, I was standing by the bus ramp going over my decision, when I bumped into Shawn.

"Where you going?" He grabbed my arm. "You remember, we 'posed to help Mr. Jenks pack up for the end of the year."

"Man, I ain't gon' help nobody."

Shawn grabbed my arm again. "You know that man gon' be mad. We just said we would stay on yesterday."

I stepped to the side to see where my bus was at, but it had pulled off. Now I had to help, I knew there was no way I could finish in time. Normally, we would all joke around, but I was quiet until he dropped us at Shawn's two hours later.

"Man, you look blowed the whole time we were helping him. What's up?"

I told him what had happened with Dion and he was shocked. "Wow, where I been at? I thought y'all were the perfect lil' light skinned couple," he said.

"Man, I'm serious, quit joking, bruh."

He still couldn't believe everything that went down, but I was glad I told him. He actually got me to laugh, which stopped me from being so mad.

"Hold up. She did what and she gave you what? Nah, bruh, you mighta asked for that one," he said, patting me on the shoulder.

"And today I'm blowed...blowed 'cause I was supposed to walk around Jasmine's house, but we were helping Jenks."

"Well, I see you moved on quick."

"Man, you know that's my homegirl."

"Dude, you sure y'all don't have nothing going on? You go around there a lot for that to be...just a friend."

I started to mention my plan, but I caught myself. "That's Malik's girl."

"Bruh, did you see what she wrote in your yearbook? Her and Malik been done for months and he broke up with her."

The more I argued with him, the more I came to my senses. "Bruh, me and Jasmine trip out all the time. She pro'lly wrote that jive in my book to get Dion and maybe to get Malik hot, too, ain't no telling. But if she really liked me, she could have been said something. You know how many times I been to her house or was up late at night talking with her? Besides, if I went with her, it would kinda be like kissing Malik, right?"

He pretended to slap me in the face. "Wrong."

"So you would go with Kalia after me?" I questioned, thinking he would say no.

"Yep, quicker than you could ask. Maybe I'd have better luck. What are you saying? You wouldn't want your friend to be happy?" He began to smile and hug on himself. "We ain't marrying these girls. We having fun; we're young."

"Well, it still ain't cool to me." *Hold up, wasn't I about to walk to her house and try to kiss her?* I guess I finally found my line and I wasn't down to cross it to find out the truth concerning Jasmine.

We had been running our mouths so much, I didn't notice how quickly we had walked from the store past Shawn's house to Malik's. Except for Steve, the whole crew was there. They were outside shooting basketball. It was one of the last times we would be together before I left for Alabama.

Malik walked up to us. "Boy, y'all missed it, the cops came 'round here for Steve with that girl mama."

Fat gave me a funny look. "I knew that was going to happen."

"He went to jail?" Shawn asked.

"Nah, they probably tried to warn him or something." Malik laughed.

"He didn't come back out though."

Shawn looked over his shoulder. "Don't tell him I told y'all, but he got burned, too."

"Gonorrhea?" Malik look disgusted. "Not Mr. Condom."

Shawn finished. "Yep, he went raw a couple times."

We all laughed.

"So Dez, you still leaving for Bama?" Malik asked.

"Yeah, I haven't talked to my mom yet, though." I leaned back against Malik's mom's car to switch the subject. "Hey, man, I know you saw what Jasmine wrote in my yearbook. You think she was for real?"

"Ah, that's old news, bruh, and it ain't for me to say. She ain't my girl." Then he shot a three pointer.

I rebounded the ball and dribbled around. "She ain't mine, neither. I thought I would ask you, though, 'fore it look foul."

He got close to stick me. "Huh, it's already foul." He reached out to stop me from shooting. "I know y'all use to write notes and stuff."

Uh oh. That caught me off guard.

"What went on after me, ain't my business." He shrugged. "Plus, I owe you for not telling you about the note me and Shawn wrote in your magazine."

My eyes lit up. "Man, I knew it was one of y'all."

Him and Shawn both backed up and laughed. "When you started going with her, we wondered if you had seen the note. Did it help?" He laughed some more.

"Yeah, it helped my year out a lot." I threw the ball at him. "Thanks."

Somehow we all ended up on the ground wrestling and talking junk 'til we got tired and laughed at everything. I was glad I hadn't gone to Jasmine's, either to make a fool of myself or to lose my homeboy's respect. Girls and friends don't mix.

"Uh oh, here come your boy, the rapper." Malik pointed as Jarvis pulled up on his sister's bike.

"What up, Dez? We gon' do these songs or what? He held up his hands. "You know, Savannah State is having their summer talent show next week. All we have to do is record a song and submit it. This is our big chance."

Did we have what it took or was it all just a dream?

CHAPTER 27

EXPRESS YOURSELF

"I'm droppin' flavor,
my behavior is hereditary
but my technique is very
necessary."

-N.W.A

Mid-June 1990

When Jarvis opened the door that Saturday morning, I couldn't help but notice the fire in his eyes.

His self-proclaimed studio, set up in his bedroom was comprised of a dual cassette deck, a keyboard, some type of beat machine, and a bootleg microphone. The feeling of hearing my voice over a beat was incredible. It was my voice, every squeaky pitch of a young boy in puberty, fighting to make his lyrics sound fresh.

Piece by piece we laid down the lyrics and I knew we had a hit.

"Yeah we just gotta' learn it." He shot me a high five.

"Well, we have about a week." I paused, "That's plenty of time, but we still need a name for our group."

The morning of the talent show, I got up early to start practicing. Then my mom came in to give a decree before she went to work. "Look, I got a few things I want you to get done today. Clean the garage out and cut the grass. I might have company tomorrow."

It's no way I'm staying home. I'd die before I miss my big chance to perform.

I thought about all the trouble I had been in this year and decided I had to say something quick.

"Mom, I have been working on this song with a friend of mine and today we are supposed to perform at Savannah State."

"A song," she looked at me to make sure I wasn't lying. "And you're just now asking me, who is the friend?"

"You know Jarvis, right?"

"No, I don't. I gotta go to work; make sure Phil talks to your friend's parents before you go."

That afternoon when Jarvis's mom dropped us off at Savannah State, it was packed. There were about fifteen performers ready to show the city what they had. All my friends came to the show, except Malik and Khalil—they had gone out of town. I was already nervous enough, but then I looked in the crowd and saw Briana. *What in the hell was she doing here?*

"Snap out of it, they're about to call us up," Jarvis yelled and wiped his hand in front of my face.

I panicked. "We never decided on a name, what did you tell them?"

"Everybody tells us that we're not old enough to do certain things, right? Well we have our dreams, and that's the start of everything. So, let's flip it and call ourselves *Young Enough*. What do you think?"

"It's better than nothing. I guess it's kind of catchy."

And with that, we were officially ready.

The announcer held the mic and screamed from the top of his lungs.

"Give it up, for two MCs called Young Enough."

Jarvis stepped in from of the crowd like it was routine. "Peace y'all, my name is J-Minister and this is my man D-EZ. We came here to cold wreck the stage."

People watched close like we had better be good. We bopped on stage to get in our zone, but when the music didn't start the crowd began to boo.

"I knew you were gonna be wack, get off the stage," a guy in the front yelled.

Jarvis jumped to the rescue and immediately pulled Fat out the crowd to beat box. "Hold up," He looked at everyone like they had better let him talk. "The sound system ain't ready, so I'ma bring up the only man I know who can start a party with his mouth. Dez, let's freestyle and show 'em what we working with." It went so smooth it almost looked rehearsed.

I nodded and after I caught the rhythm Fat was freaking, I began.

"Savannah State you don't have to wait
Point me to the stage, I'll show I'm great
I get up in ya ear like a Q-tip...
For the cute girls check how I flip my lips."

I kept spittin' until Jarvis jumped in to flow. Now that we had their undivided attention, it was time to really set it off.

"DJ Art La Rock, you ready," Jarvis yelled out to the DJ in charge of the talent show.

After a couple of dope scratches our song finally dropped and we started our routine with the chorus.

We're from G-A and it's like that
make em clap clap, make em clap clap
We're from G-A and it's like that
Make 'em clap clap, make 'em clap clap

Jarvis started:

Amazing, yeah I know you've been waitin'
When I don't rap, it's like I'm suffocatin'
head of our time... y'all play catch up
on your mark, I make the crowd erupt
Ask Pat Prokop, to predict the hit
Strike, I'm lightning, Call me Mic Tyson
Ever get a chance to flow, you make it count
People come, dance and get off the couch

Then I jumped in:

I'm a young fella', soon to be, best sella'
better tell her, we stand like Mandela'
The boaster, microphones in my holster

FLICTED

D-E-Z, on ya bedroom poster
Expression is the weapon we chose, our views
Give it to you raw, this is not the news.
For years they been talkin' bout down south
like we can't rap, sucka put this in ya mouth.

I had never felt anything like it. Two hundred people were clapping and pumping their fists out of control. After we spit the chorus, I put one finger in the air and just soaked it all in. *We're from G-A and it's like that...*

"Y'all killed it." Fat threw his arm around me while the announcer called out our name for another round of applause.

"Thanks, man, you saved us, that beat box you did was incredible."

While everyone was beyond hyped, I examined Briana again. My eyes had never really left her and I knew she loved the performance. After I got off stage, I cut through the crowd to talk to her.

"What are you doing here?" I placed my hands on her shoulders. "How did you know about the show?"

"Okay, this is crazy," she started. "I bumped into Malik at the grocery store yesterday and he told me you were performing. Plus, the girl in the singing group goes to my church, so I begged my dad to bring me." She turned and waved to her dad who was leaning up against the back wall.

Then, she folded her hands over her chest and stared at me for a moment. "I loved it; I didn't realize you were that good."

I knew my feelings for her were showing and it was no use in hiding it. "Hey, I have something I want to ask you." I paused. I tried hard not to stutter, but I still tripped over a couple syllables. "Briana, I wa…wanted to know if you ever… liked me?"

"Like you, of course I like you." She tapped on my head as if I were dumb for asking. "We've been cool for awhile now."

I looked into her eyes. *Get it together, Dez.* "No, I mean *like* me, as in — did you ever want to be my girl?"

She slammed the brakes on her laughter and talked as if she could see straight through me. "Of course I did, but you knew that." She tapped my head again. "But hey, I wasn't good enough, remember?"

I could feel my Adam's apple turn into a cantaloupe. That truth was hard to swallow.

I tried to apologize and explain a bit, but it came out all wrong. *Could I tell her exactly why I had chosen Kalia? Hell no.*

"Look, before you think you have to say something else," she put her hand up in front of my face, "I'm not about to go with you after those other girls. I like you as a friend. I know you love music and I wanted to see you perform before you left town. You don't owe me anything."

After that, I couldn't say a thing. She had officially read me my rights.

While Jarvis and everyone else remained hyped, I had taken yet another loss. On top of that, we didn't win. The next couple of groups sang incredibly. Still, no one could take that moment from us. We had arrived.

Later that day, I was cleaning up the garage and playing the song we recorded when my mom pulled up.

"Why do you have that up so loud?" She got out of the car like she was tired. "Hold up is that you?" She glanced over at my radio.

"How could you tell?" I asked.

"Boy, I know your voice; I gave birth to you, didn't I?" We hadn't talked much since the gun incident, but I knew we needed to. After I finished cutting the grass in the dark, I came inside.

"I didn't know you were trying to make songs," she said as she finished cooking dinner. "Did you know I used to sing?"

"Sing?" The only thing I could think of was that opera jive she did. I hoped she wasn't about to give me an example.

"Man, I tell you," she reminisced. "I would make stuff up in my head and sing all the time growing up. Music just came in my head and I would make up words to what I heard."

"Hold up. You wanted to be a real professional singer?" I asked in disbelief. My mom had never shared anything she wanted to be with me, so I was listening intently as she continued.

"Yeah, I told you before when I was about twelve, I left Savannah and moved to Philadelphia 'cause my auntie wanted to help me with my schooling. Well, while I was there she taught me how to sing. She really wanted me to make it, but I was too shy. I just couldn't…do it in front of people. But, I had a chance to see and experience things a little girl from West Savannah wouldn't normally get to do in the 1950's. My auntie had a great, big old piano in her house and she would play it while I learned to sing."

I looked confused. "Why didn't you try after you got older?"

"You know...I don't know. I just let it go." She sat down. "Next thing you know, I was married with two children and a whole lot of responsibilities."

Since we were finally talking again, I thought it would be a good time to mention Alabama.

"Mama, how do you feel about me staying with my dad next year for school?"

"For the whole year?" she asked, surprised.

I sat down across from her. "Is that okay?"

"I don't mind, if that's what you want to do. You don't want to go 'cause of me and ya' stepdad, is it? 'Cause we're okay. We had some issues, but things will get better," she reassured me.

"Nah, it's just that I've been living with you my whole life. I think it would be cool to be around Dad some more. I'm not mad about anything."

"Okay, if that's what you want, I'll give your dad a call. Just promise me you're going to do good in school."

"Of course," I promised.

"Don't throw your gifts away. You're smart and you have always been bright. Did you know you could read at three? I mean actually read, like you were six or seven years old. People were shocked when they heard you. For that, I'll always praise God. Hearing you read stopped me from worrying that you'd turn out like me. I used to look at you running around the house and I said, 'Lord, what am I gon' do with this little boy?'"

I waved my hand to interrupt her. "Hold up. What do you mean... like you?"

"I mean, with my reading and all. Hand me that bill on the table." She opened up the letter from the power company. "When I ask you to read for me, it's not because I just want you to. It's because it's hard for me. I see things backwards or jumbled up." She held up the letter inside. "See how the paper says Savannah Electric? If I don't concentrate and take my time, it will look like something totally different." She looked down at the floor and then to the ceiling.

"Now, growing up, all I heard was, 'Old dumb Red can't read to save her life.' I remember the teacher would write my name on the board and point to it and I couldn't say what it was. Just imagine how I felt when all the other kids could." She stretched her arms to regain her strength.

"Son, I held on to a lot of pain," she continued. "I used to walk around and dream that I could paint myself with black tar to be dark-skinned and that I could read. But no matter how hard I tried, I couldn't."

I was so shocked that I didn't know what to say. My mom had never talked to me in this way. These details were pieces of her soul unfolding. It explained a lot about her and the anger I sometimes felt from her but didn't understand. I was frozen in thought, and at 14, I couldn't even process it all.

"So, are you... okay?" I finally asked.

"Yeah, I'm okay, son. Life deals us all a hand and we have to make the best of it. At least, in Philly, I found out I wasn't dumb. My auntie tried to help me. She really did. She thought I was just slow at first, but when I couldn't keep up, she took me to a doctor."

Then, she recalled for me the scene in the doctor's office:

"Slow?" the doctor said. "This child isn't slow. She has a condition. She's afflicted with dyslexia."

"Dis who? I didn't know what the heck that meant so I asked him, do you mean I'm flicted?" my mama said.

"Flic...are you trying to say afflicted?" He smiled and said very kindly to me. "Yes, you are afflicted, you have an affliction."

When she said that, I looked at my mom like I was looking at myself. As a child, I viewed her as the lady I lived with who yelled and complained; but for the first time in a long time, I knew I loved and respected her.

This word flicted had opened an understanding; a door into the past and future. The pain carried from parent to child, from one generation to the next, from mistakes to curses. We often miss things when we take life at just face value, but there's always more to it than what it seems to be.

The talk with my mother reminded me of a sermon I once heard: If you train a child up in the way they should go, when they get old they won't depart from it.

This year had put that scripture to the test. We were all blessed. Our lives were not perfect. However, I can see how our parents gave us the best they could. Everyone's parents, among the people that I knew, worked and put us in an environment where we could be successful. The rest was up to us.

****

A week later, on the day I was to leave, I hugged my mom and picked up my bags. I took one last look around my room and thought about how everything was going to change. *What a year.* My dad called out from the front door, "Hey son, are you ready?"

FLICTED

As I stepped outside in the hot Savannah sun, I smiled at my mom and made my way to the car. Then, I heard the phone faintly ringing while I put my last bag in the trunk with all my music.

"Heeey Dez," she called out. "The phone is for you." My face wrinkled up. *Everyone knows I'm leaving. Who could it be?* "Who is it, mama?"

"Some girl, I think she said her name was... Briana..."

EPILOGUE

Thirty years later, living in Atlanta, I was driving back from Jarvis's house after working on a beat for the rappers, Gucci Mane and Big Krit. The pride and recognition we wanted to see in the south had come and then some. Since 1994, the group, OutKast had put our state on the map with flows that were legendary. One half of that duo, Big Boi was from Savannah. Then in 2001, the young rapper, Camoflauge gave our city another nationally recognized hip-hop star.

We had talked about the good old days and all the songs we recorded when we were younger. Then he mentioned how flicted I was when he met me back in 1989. I hadn't heard that word in a long time, but it triggered many events from childhood. I laughed and thought of all the crazy times I remembered in middle school.

The teenage experience is not an easy one. What if I had slept with that crack head? What if I took that gun to school? What if those cops had shot us? What if I had chosen Briana over Kalia? As I drove down the highway, I looked back on this time as a steppingstone into manhood. Many didn't get the opportunity I had to learn from mistakes. I made it and through music I had an opportunity to help inspire others.

Before going inside my house, I let the window down and put the first CD I recorded in. Every track on that CD was my life... and it sounded as a good as the first day I wrote it.

Made in the USA
Columbia, SC
07 July 2018